what you are now enjoying

what you are now enjoying

stories

Sarah Gerkensmeyer

AUTUMN
HOUSE PRESS
pittsburgh

"Autumn House" and "Autumn House Press" are registered trademarks
owned by Autumn House Press, a nonprofit corporation whose mission is the
publication and promotion of poetry and other fine literature.

Autumn House Press receives state arts funding support through
a grant from the Pennsylvania Council on the Arts, a state agency
funded by the Commonwealth of Pennsylvania, and the National
Endowment for the Arts, a federal agency.

ISBN: 978-1-932870-80-0

Library of Congress Control Number: 2012920849

for my boys

contents

what you are now enjoying

what you are now enjoying

JAN IS SURPRISED by how easy it is to find a parking spot. *This is a good sign,* she thinks.

When she walks into the lobby, the placement officer, a pale woman with nice teeth, hands the baby to Jan before she even has a chance to sit down. Immediately, the placement officer begins to unbutton Jan's blouse.

"You remembered to wear the right kind of shirt," the woman says, moving quickly. "You've been taking your vitamins, I'm sure."

And then the baby is pressed there against Jan, skin to skin. The baby knows what to do and does not hesitate. Jan has never breastfed before. Her right breast grows warm. She lets herself look down and catches a quick glimpse of a few shiny, almost translucent tufts of hair. Somehow she knows that it is a boy.

Jan looks around the little lobby, a room full of spidery, thriving plants. She is surprised when she realizes that she is alone. The placement officer has disappeared. Jan guesses that she is behind the door with the sign that reads, "Personnel Only Please." Jan stares at the empty chair across from her and tries to remember exactly what the counselor had told them during their first few group sessions. She had said something about a moment of surprise, followed by a numb sensation all over. She had mentioned release, and circulation.

Jan notices two things:

1. Her left eye has stopped twitching.
2. She knows that she is going to be a little late to work that morning, and she doesn't care.

JAN had been getting headaches for the past year. The throbbing would start at the back of her skull, a dull film of pain. Within an hour, sometimes within fifteen minutes, it would settle up in her forehead, chiseling away at her thoughts, even her speech.

"Stress related," Jan's doctor told her. "Common for women your age."

He gave her a prescription for huge blue pills that made her throat ache and shut her down completely for at least half a day.

At work, late in the afternoon, Jan would sit at her desk and wait to feel the almost imperceptible throb start at the back of her head. She'd watch her screensaver, animated ducklings on a pond, and listen for the footsteps of her supervisor behind her. She was ready to pick up the phone and dial a random extension in an instant, or to press ENTER on her keyboard so that a spreadsheet or an interoffice memo would pop up and make the idle ducklings disappear.

Jan had no idea what she wanted to do with her life. She'd get a ticklish feeling in her head when she tried to concentrate and think through her options. She felt silly. A couple years after college, she had realized that the future wasn't simply there, a tall man in a nice pinstriped suit waiting outside the door of her tiny studio apartment holding out a shiny new briefcase for her to cling to, a neat family. Now when she looked at herself in a mirror she noticed dull hair, okay skin, bright-ish eyes. She looked like she was on the verge of pulling herself together. She had looked like this for the past six years.

"WHAT'S that noise?" Jan's mother asks when she calls one night, a couple days after Jan's visit to the placement agency.

"What noise?"

"Is that static?" her mother asks. "Do you have the TV on?"

Jan realizes that her mother can hear him breastfeeding, the wash of soft suckling just below the phone.

"Jan?"

"That's nothing," Jan says.

"Okay," her mother says.

Normally this would agitate Jan—a phone call with her mother full of awkward silences. But she feels okay. She feels calm.

"You should come for a visit," Jan says suddenly.

She is full of surprises.

"Okay," her mother says.

Jan imagines her mother, just one state away, listening to the mysterious murmur coming from the other end of the line. She looks down and glimpses the top of his little head. She feels fine. Jan decides to write a letter to her mother and tell her that way, not over the phone. The letter is short and to the point. She doesn't want to make a big deal out of anything. She mails it the next day.

BEFORE they started going to the group therapy sessions, Jan and her girlfriends would meet for drinks a couple times a week. They'd find each other after five in a dark bar downtown. They'd order something strong and stare at one another's doughy skin, which was flaccid and unremarkable in the dim bar, zapped from an entire day of fluorescent lighting.

"I'm tired," Jan said on a cold Wednesday a few months back.

It was five thirty and they were all there, crammed into a booth, warming each other.

"I'm tired, too," Nina said, her huge eyes peeking beneath heavy lids.

They were always tired. And they always talked about how tired they were. They drank, and yawned, and then went home. But instead of sitting there that particular early evening and nodding, they started to talk about exactly what kind of tired they were. Jan told them about her headaches, which her friends knew about, but she really described them for the first time. Nina talked about the acidic knots in her stomach that jumped into her throat when she was nervous at work. Which was often. She shuddered when she described the sensation, looking down at her little wrists.

"It's like trying to swallow fire," she said.

Danni was quiet. She ordered a shot of tequila. Her thick hair was pulled back into a haphazard, beautiful mess of knots and twists. She started to yawn and then stopped, forcing tears to the edges of her eyes. Danni told them about the tiny lump in her right breast. She had noticed it three weeks before. Her doctor didn't think a biopsy was necessary.

"He says it's stress," she said. "Something fibrous."

And they all nodded to make it true.

They ordered more drinks and stayed too late for a weeknight.

"Look at us," Jan said, holding up a shot of tequila, closing her eyes. "We're stuck." She threw her head back and took the shot. "We're stuck for some reason."

Her friends smiled at her. Even Danni, whom she was scared for.

Jan got a call from Nina the next day, well before lunch. The three of them usually didn't call each other at work until late afternoon had rolled around, when they were all sitting at their desks feeling something slow pull at them from the inside. Nina had found a website.

"We're perfect for this type of therapy," she told Jan, explaining that group sessions were about to start in a Lutheran church basement on Wednesday nights, a few streets over from where they usually met for drinks.

This type of therapy was becoming quite common. Jan knew of women who had undergone similar treatment. A couple of them worked a few floors below her in acquisitions. She'd seen them at the small Greek café across the street during lunch and noticed a little glow, a looseness in their shoulders. She had wondered if it was forced.

"I'll try it," Jan told Nina.

Nina called Danni next. And for the rest of the day they kept calling each other, the red light blinking on Jan's phone. She used her office voice and spoke in short sentences. Even though she was excited, she managed to sound professional. She laughed a little, but it was the low, hollow office laugh that slips below the radar.

WHEN Jan is switching breasts, he gets a lost look in his eyes. His fists search the air. He squints at the ceiling. But it doesn't take long. Jan is a fast learner. They both get settled. Jan's feet and hands grow warm.

AT the fifth meeting, a couple weeks before each woman was assigned a baby, they had learned about how breast milk is a live, biological fluid. Jan couldn't help thinking about tide pools, about all the rubbery, salty things she had seen while poking around with a stick when she was on vacation at the shore as a kid. They learned about living immune cells. Jan started to have second thoughts. But then they were fitted for the harnesses. Jan was surprised by how natural it felt after all the straps had been adjusted and the Velcro pulled into place. A hollow hammock rested just below her breasts. The counselor filled each woman's empty pouch with oranges. They practiced walking around. Sitting and standing up. Jan, Nina, and Danni huddled next to the doorway, ignoring the cold air washing in from the empty linoleum hall. The three of them giggled and tried to lift their shoulders. Jan wanted to ask them if they were really going to go through with it. They looked at one another, at the lumpy hammocks hanging below their breasts, and breathed in the surprising smell of citrus.

JAN doesn't get frustrated this morning when the line at Starbucks is stretched out the door. She doesn't glare at the retreating figure of her supervisor after he tells her that her report on last month's sales deficits, which he hadn't told her about until that exact moment, is late. She doesn't watch the clock all day. She takes an hour-and-a-half for lunch. The sky is bluer. She calls Nina on her way home.

"This works," she says.

"I know."

Nina's voice is husky. For a moment, Jan doesn't think that it can be her. The traffic is horrible. Jan doesn't care.

"I'm going to go for a jog," Nina says. "I feel like I could run a hundred miles."

A car honks somewhere behind Jan. The sun slices through the windshield and into her eyes. She listens to his little nestling sounds. One of his weak fists presses into her left breast. Her right foot is easy on the brake pedal. Patient. There is no need to hurry.

WHILE walking down the soup aisle at the grocery store, while switching from the left lane into the right lane on an empty highway, while sleeping, Jan will forget that he is there. Then she'll walk past the long mirror in her downstairs hallway and see a little hand floating there near her chest. She'll rest her index finger in his palm, and he'll hold on for a while before she tucks him back in.

People know what's under there. Like it's any big surprise. Some people do stare. Jan's Pilates instructor seems uncertain. Her hairdresser gives her a look, and Jan wonders if she is worried about the chemicals. People know he's not hers, the way she covers him up like that with her special mail-order shirts. They know she is in therapy. She watches strangers glance at the bundle resting beneath her chest and then try to diagnose her in their minds. Performance anxiety. Social anxiety. Post traumatic stress disorder. With that one, they try to guess exactly what happened, why it was so traumatic. She was the only survivor of a horrible fire, or her father killed her mother with an axe. If Jan eats too much spicy food, he makes a lot more noise than usual and most everyone notices the hump of his little body then.

Jan sees other women with the telltale swell beneath their shirts. She does it, too: stares at them and starts firing away silently, disorder after disorder.

THERE are nine women in Jan's support group, which still meets every week in the church basement after each woman has been paired up with a nursing baby. The sessions are different now. Everyone is calm and quiet. When someone speaks, there is that constant wash of suckling in the background, a soft chorus.

Jan doesn't need the sessions like she used to. She could stop going and be perfectly fine. But the room is full of happy women, most of them young like her and her girlfriends. She likes seeing the different bundles, little legs and arms sometimes escaping and moving about in the quiet. When it is her turn to talk about how things are going, Jan is honest. The first few sessions, before they were matched up with the babies, Jan had lied and said that she was pretty happy, not too stressed, not worried about whether or not she would meet a man who didn't smoke or if she would receive a raise to help with the payments on her tiny house. Danni and Nina would lift their eyebrows a little bit, but they lied, too. Now Jan says the same exact things and she means them. She breathes deeply and then says that she doesn't care how old she is when she gets married. Maybe she won't ever get married. She feels buzzed when she says this.

Jan and her friends had been caught off guard the first time they came to a session and found medical equipment spread about the church basement, a couple nurses in T-shirts and jeans waiting to take their blood. None of this had been mentioned on the website Nina had found. But it turned out the tests weren't a big deal. A little pressure here, a little prick there. Jan hugged the bundle beneath her chest with her left arm while one of the nurses took blood out of her other arm. He was warm there against her, and she relaxed. When the counselor asked Jan to talk about a stressful situation that had happened that week at a local campground during a work retreat that was supposed to promote teamwork and morale, her blood pressure did not spike. The nurse who was monitoring Jan's vitals gave her a little thumbs-up.

Sandra, the oldest of the group, talked about her divorce. One of the nurses took her blood pressure right after and gave her a thumbs-up. Kayla, a shy woman with gray skin that had turned vibrant over the past few weeks, told the group for the first time about how her uncle had abused her as a child. She got a thumbs-up, too. Danni talked about how she has felt a little empty and directionless ever since graduate school. She didn't cry. One nurse held a stethoscope up to Danni's back and had her breathe deeply while the other one probed gently at her breasts, just above the baby's head, her cold nurse hand lost inside Danni's shirt. When the nurses were done, they both gave Danni a thumbs-up. Jan locked eyes with Nina. A double thumbs-up. Jan's relief was very loose and wishy-washy. Like things could possibly turn out any other way.

JAN'S mother makes a big deal during her visit. Her suitcase is full of clothes for him. Little striped jumpers with choo choo trains and lions. Jan shows her mother the white onesies in her underwear drawer.

"I've got plenty, no matter how big he gets," she says.

Jan's mother ignores her and stuffs the jumpers and miniature Levis in next to Jan's socks.

When Jan pushes her mother's hands away—she has been grabbing at him the entire visit, trying to pull out his head, a little arm—her mother apologizes and gets sentimental.

"I just remember how it was with you. This type of situation didn't exist back then."

"Therapy," Jan says.

Her mother looks at her.

"This type of therapy," Jan says.

Jan takes her mother to the new art gallery downtown, all experimental stuff. They eat out a lot. They go for walks. Jan takes Monday off at work, which is the day before her mother leaves, and they go to the zoo. It is a gray, quiet day. The air feels wet.

Jan notices her mother's eyes tracing the bulge beneath her shirt every few minutes. Her mother stops her next to the kangaroos and says, "I can't help thinking we are here because of him. So that he can enjoy this." She swings her left arm, a vague gesture that covers the entire expanse of the little zoo.

"You know better than that," Jan says. "He can't see a thing."

He is covered completely, lost in the folds of one of Jan's special shirts.

Jan's mother gets teary, and Jan is annoyed. But she's okay. A few months before, Jan would have gotten worked up, said something nasty, gone out to her car and left her mother standing there in front of the weathered plaque on marsupials. Instead, Jan smiles for her mother. There isn't any fight in her.

"Have I told you about my HDL cholesterol levels?" Jan asks. "I can't believe I haven't told you about that yet."

Jan's mother stares at the kangaroos, the tears in her eyes glistening like mad. Jan sighs and takes one of her mother's hands, placing it on the bundle below her chest. She lets go and her mother's hand stays there, pressed into the back of the baby's little head, trying to feel him through the cotton of Jan's shirt.

"Don't you feel sad?" her mother asks.

"What do you mean?"

Jan's mother doesn't say anything else. She just stares at her hand, and Jan lets her keep it there until the tears go away. Jan ignores the irony of how they are standing in front of the marsupial exhibit while all of this happens. She doesn't let this piss her off. Her mother, thank God, doesn't point it out anyway.

JAN decides to paint her kitchen the color of limes. She calls in sick two days in a row in order to finish it. She misses an important meeting on expanding into upper class markets. The walls need four coats of paint. She is patient and lets them dry completely between coats. Her head is light. She drinks tea and stares out her kitchen window at the dull-looking brown birds poking around in the grass. When she realizes that she needs another can of paint, she goes out to her car, gets in, and fastens her seatbelt. For the first time, she notices the tighter fit with the baby snug there against her chest. She likes it. She feels safer.

ONE night the counselor talks about the benefits of breast feeding, besides the psychological ones that brought this group of women together. She talks about how breastfeeding is a form of birth control. She talks about how milk production burns up to five hundred calories a day. She says it's like swimming thirty laps or riding a bicycle uphill for over an hour.

The counselor keeps listing things and Jan zones out. She closes her eyes and pretends that they aren't sitting in folding chairs down in the basement off of the church kitchen. She imagines that they are up in the sanctuary and a few candles are lit. Jan doesn't even have to listen. She feels whole. If they were in the sanctuary, Jan could stare up at Jesus' face, which would be floating above the counselor, his wooden arms spread wide. He'd be looking down at all of them. Jan does not know what to think about Jesus, about God. That doesn't bother her. Not right now.

JAN, Nina, and Danni avoid the bars and meet at each other's places instead. They end up spread out on one of their beds, a bottle of red wine on a nightstand or a bookcase.

"Can I feel for the lump?" Nina asks Danni one night when they are at Jan's house.

It has been a couple weeks since the double thumbs-up from the nurses. Nina looks nervous, and at first Jan thinks she is embarrassed to feel Danni's breasts. But then she realizes that Nina is scared to discover something, to feel a little lump that the nurse's professional fingers couldn't find.

Danni sets her wine glass down on the floor.

"Press with the pads of your fingers," she says.

When she lifts up her shirt, Jan gets a good look at the baby girl that Danni was matched up with and notices that she has wide eyes, a hairline that hasn't filled in yet. Nina reaches past the baby and gently pushes into the breast that Danni is feeding with. The baby doesn't seem to mind. She keeps feeding.

Jan is lucky. The baby she was given suckles even when he's asleep. The counselor calls this "ghost suckling," when the babies go through the motions while they aren't feeding. Some of the women in the group complain about when their babies fall asleep and stop suckling. There will be a sudden spike in their moods at the worst possible moments. During an important conference call, or just after sex.

"There's nothing," Nina says, absently running her hand over the baby girl's head before helping Danni pull her shirt back down.

"Nothing to worry about at all," Danni says.

They stay up late and order Indian takeout. Jan wishes that her two friends could stay there, spread out on top of her bed forever. They could eat an eternity of butter chicken and garlic naan bread. That could be it for the rest of Jan's days.

WHEN Jan changes his diaper he watches the shadows on the ceiling, if there are any. He gets cold easily, but he is patient and fusses rarely. They make eye contact from time to time, and Jan can't help thinking that he is shy. She snaps him back into his onesie. She smiles at him a little. He watches her and there is a soft punch in her chest. Something like recognition. It isn't unpleasant.

NINA is sitting there on the church steps, waiting below the red double doors, when Jan and Danni arrive for the next meeting.

"I'm not going in," Nina says, her hands stretched out stiffly on her knees.

Jan and Danni sit on either side of her.

"I started to feel weird about it," Nina says.

There's an edge of panic in her voice. Jan turns slowly and looks at Nina's shirt, a tight-fitting black turtleneck that hugs her breasts and falls straight and flat against her ribcage and abdomen. Nina looks like a scarecrow, like her stuffing has been ripped out.

"You took him back," Jan says.

Danni shakes her head at Nina in slow motion, her hair full of life and bounce.

"I felt like there were so many questions I should ask when I took him back to the agency," Nina says.

"Like what?" Danni asks.

"I don't know," Nina says. "About what would happen to him, I guess. Aren't you curious?"

Jan shrugs. Her shoulders feel strong. She watches Nina stare at her and Danni. Nina is jumpy and can't sit still. Her breathing is hard. She looks hungry staring at them like that. And Jan just shrugs. She can't help it.

JAN goes to a bar alone, something she would have never done before. She does not feel lost or desperate. Nothing feels forced. A man—early thirties, nice arms—sits next to her.

"Buy you a drink?" he asks. But then he glances down at the swell beneath her chest.

"Moderation is key," Jan says, smiling.

She's drunk already and she orders herself another drink, ignoring the man's offer and the hesitation that had followed it. The man smiles with his eyes and his forehead, careful to keep his gaze on Jan's face. He pulls out a cigarette. Another smoker. Jan doesn't care. There is no collapse in her heart, no *Of course*. There's just that warm glow deep in her belly, pushing up toward her chin.

They don't say much to each other. The silence between them is hopeless and dead, but Jan does not feel awkward. The man starts to look around the room, inhaling his smoke.

Before Jan leaves, she places her elbows up on the sticky bar and her chest feels weightless. She thinks about kissing the stranger next to her but doesn't. In the car, she listens to the motivational CD the placement officer had given her when she picked up the baby at the agency. "There is no happiness equal to what you are now enjoying," a woman's voice says. Jan drives home slowly while thinking about that.

"I COULD be an interior decorator," Jan tells her mother one night over the phone.

"Yes. You could," her mother says.

"I could specialize in a particular type of room. Like bedrooms. Or the kitchen."

Jan's mother says, "You've always had an eye for color."

The two of them have been talking on the phone every day. Jan finds herself telling her mother things she would have never considered sharing with her before. They talk about Jan's credit card debt, about the possibility of refinishing her basement. Her mother seems genuinely supportive. She brings up things like Jan's "eye for color," things Jan has never heard her mention before.

"I've started taking Pilates classes," Jan's mother tells her.

"That's good," Jan says.

She feels like she's on autopilot when she speaks with her mother. Like there's a tiny, gentle motor whirring in her head and she doesn't have to do a thing to manage it. Jan's mother hasn't mentioned the situation with the baby since her visit. *She has gotten over it,* Jan thinks.

NINA comes over to spend a rainy Saturday afternoon in Jan's kitchen. They bake cranberry orange muffins. Nina eats a few in a row and Jan can't help staring.

"What?" Nina asks, her mouth full.

She has gained weight over the past couple of weeks, since she stopped the therapy. Her cheeks have grown rounder.

"You're hungry," Jan says. "That's all."

"I'm starving," Nina says, tearing the crisp crust off a muffin, watching the sweet-smelling steam escape.

She gets restless once she stops eating. She brushes her hand along the counter as if she might clean up the crumbs. She makes more of a mess.

"It's like when I quit smoking," Nina says. "I don't know what to do with my hands."

Jan looks at her own hands, which are folded in her lap.

"But you weren't using your hands that much before," she says.

"That doesn't matter."

Nina stands up and walks over to the window above the sink. She holds her shoulders up near her ears, as if she has been hurt or insulted.

Jan needs to change the baby's diaper, but she doesn't want to leave Nina alone in the kitchen staring out at the little side yard like that. She grabs a diaper and wipes from the bathroom and comes back into the kitchen where she lays him gently on the floor. Nina turns around. Jan can feel her watching.

"I want to hold him," Nina says.

"Sure."

"Just for a minute," Nina says.

"That's fine."

Nina kneels down and looks at him for a few moments before picking him up. She faces him away from her and lassoes her arms beneath his legs, like a swing. She walks him over to the window so that he can gaze out at nothing.

Jan doesn't like Nina holding him. She feels like he is ten miles away from her, lost, out of her sight. Nina turns around and faces Jan. She moves the baby into the crook of her arm and looks down at his face. He waves his arm at her. He's hungry. Nina must still be producing milk. There must be a throbbing in her breasts, an irresistible longing. For a flash moment, Jan considers letting Nina feed him, a quick pick-me-up. But it is a fleeting, wild thought. She walks over to Nina and takes him back, slips him inside the harness, covers him with her shirt.

Nina walks back over to the muffins and stares at them. Then she looks up and Jan can tell that she is disappointed, that she is desperate. She can tell that they had shared the same exact thought. Nina knows what Jan had almost offered her. She knows that Jan had considered it for two seconds, three at the most.

JAN'S mother comes out for another visit. Even though it's just a four hour drive, they only see one another a couple times a year. This is the second visit in two months. Jan doesn't push herself to make sure her place is spotless. She doesn't pick up special teas and biscuits from the co-op down the street from work. Her mother doesn't notice. She is full of energy and smiles when she gets there late on a Thursday night. They talk for a couple of hours before going to bed. When Jan wakes in the morning to get ready for work, her mother has started a pot of coffee. She has made waffles. She has brought a yellow fruit bowl for Jan's freshly painted kitchen.

Jan invites Danni and Nina over that night. Her mother makes pasta. She gets tipsy before the water has boiled. Her jeans are too tight. Danni loves Jan's mother. She tells her about the tiny lump in her breast. Her eyes get teary when she explains that it has gone away.

"For good," she says.

"That's amazing," Jan's mother says. "But it makes complete sense." She glances at Danni's breasts, at the mound resting just beneath them. "Nature's way of healing," she says, smiling, her eyes a little wild.

Jan thinks it's the excitement of being surrounded by young women, by friends. She doesn't recognize her mother—the tight little sweater and the quick gestures and words.

Nina looks like she's pouting a bit during dinner. She eats quickly and then keeps her arms crossed over her chest after she has finished.

"How much longer do you think you'll need her?" Nina asks Danni, nodding at her breasts.

"Who knows," Danni says. "Things are going so well."

"Didn't you say your back has been bothering you?" Nina asks, sitting up in her chair.

"We've been doing exercises," Jan says. "They started teaching them to us last Wednesday night."

Nina is such a petite woman, but Jan is sure that the exercises would have made her more comfortable and given her the strength to carry around the growing weight. She looks at Nina and watches her face grow red.

"Are you okay?" Jan asks her.

"Yes," Nina says, her face even hotter. "We're all okay, don't you think? Isn't all of this a bit unnecessary? Don't you feel strange?"

Jan and Danni don't say anything. Nina glares at their chests. Jan feels like laughing out loud. She feels bad for Nina, but she can't believe how worked up she is. She avoids looking at Danni, because maybe they'll both laugh. Then Jan thinks of the moment in her kitchen a few days ago, when Nina was holding him. Jan feels like they have a secret, one that they could never tell Danni.

Nina tells Jan's mother that it was nice meeting her. She seems embarrassed when she leaves. Jan walks her out to her car and puts a hand on her shoulder. Nina rolls it off when she reaches into her pocket for her car keys. She looks naked without even a purse.

"You could try again," Jan says. "They could give you a different baby, I'm sure."

"Don't say that," Nina says, her face flat.

She jerks at her car door and then sits there in the front seat with her feet still outside the car, crushed into the gravel in Jan's driveway. Her hair has become dry and limp and is pressed flat against her skull.

"I just wish you could think about it a little bit," she says. "Or I wish I hadn't started thinking about it, or worrying about it. Whatever this is."

Nina juts her chin out at Jan's chest with the word "this." And then she pulls her feet into her car and slams the door and shoves her key into the ignition. She moves so quickly now. Jan can't remember if it was always that way.

When Jan gets back inside, her mother and Danni are sitting conspiratorially close on the couch. Jan's mother looks at her. She is smoking, something Jan does not allow in her house.

"She's just in withdrawal, honey," her mother says, exhaling. "She's going to be fine. You'll see."

And even though this is not at all like Jan's mother—this softness in her eyes, this sudden understanding—Jan does not care. She nods and smiles. She sits and pushes herself closer to her mother. She lets her head and shoulders sink back into the cushions, smoke dancing in front of her face. People change, she decides, listening to the soft nestling noises coming up from beneath her shirt, and from beneath Danni's. People change, and that's just fine with her.

JAN wakes up in the middle of the night. She is a heavy sleeper and she can't figure out what has woken her. Is she hungry? Thirsty? She rolls onto her back and closes her eyes. She tries to fall back asleep. Her arms feel heavy. Her feet are cold. She hears a car drive by her house and worries suddenly about whether or not she had locked the backdoor before going to bed.

There is an ache when she realizes what is missing. It is that simple. She does not sit up in bed and gasp. She does not rip at the front of her shirt. She stays there, motionless on her back, for several minutes. Next she sits on the edge of her bed, rubbing her arms. The ache is faint but steady, spreading out from her chest to the tips of her fingers. Jan can't help thinking of Nina, her arms crossed over her chest during dinner.

She is not surprised when she turns on the light in the guest bedroom and sees that all of her mother's things are gone. She flips on the porch light and sees that the driveway is also empty.

The drive to her mother's house does not seem long. Her hands on the wheel feel awkward and her feet are sluggish, but when Jan pulls into her mother's driveway a couple hours after the sun has risen, she feels like she has gotten there all too quickly. She stares at her mother's garage for a few minutes. She waits until she feels warmth spread up from her neck and into her face. *I am angry,* Jan thinks. *I am upset.* She feels self-conscious, as if she has borrowed someone else's feelings. She stares at herself in the rearview mirror and watches a hesitant flush fill her cheeks. *I am extremely angry.* The sensation is like a small pond thawing, like déjà vu. When Jan doesn't feel like she's acting, when the pulse in her temple feels real, she gets out of her car and walks to her mother's front door.

Jan doesn't bother knocking. She knows where she'll find her mother. In the back of the house, in the kitchen, her mother is sitting there at the table with the newspaper spread out before her, a baby bottle set on top of Arts and Entertainment. He is in her arms.

"My little dough lump," Jan's mother says, placing her chin on top of his head.

He is wearing a blue jumper with a brown walrus across his chest. His hair is still wispy, still translucent. His eyes are wide and focused. Jan had expected him to look blind and pale, stunned. He is pleased, staring at her with his silvery bright eyes.

"You're just tired," Jan's mother says.

She bops him lightly a couple times on her knee and then pulls him back against her, as if she's had a second thought.

"There's nothing wrong with you, honey," she says. "You're just lonely. I remember being twenty-something, and then thirty-something. And feeling lost."

There is still that weird quality to her mother's voice, a plasticity that has never been there before. But Jan knows that her mother is being perfectly straightforward now. She has gotten what she wants.

"Nina is right," Jan's mother says, pushing him into the crook of her arm, rocking him. "It's unnatural what you girls were doing. Therapy or not. It's strange and it's wrong."

Jan can't stop looking at him. His hands are folded low on his belly, like an old man. He watches her. The clock in the kitchen tocks. The ache in her chest tocks right along with it. This is where she grew up.

"My little dough lump," Jan's mother says again, firmly this time. A challenge.

And then there is the bottle. Jan's mother holds it up to his lips. He hesitates. He won't take it. He tries to push it away from his face. But Jan's mother is persistent. She knows how to wait things out. She knows how to stay calm. A few minutes pass. He cries and shakes his head. Jan is anxious. She feels like she should do something. Her old life rushes back at her—the status quo, the mundane, the deep, empty lake—and she just stands there.

She doesn't hear him when he's making all that fuss. She focuses only on the sounds he makes once he has given up, once he is satisfied with the warm, tough nipple pressed between his lips. There is that: the crisp, rubbery sound of him pulling at his bottle, perfectly content.

For the first time, Jan lets herself think about where he came from. She tries to imagine all of the babies. Are they kept together in a big room, in matching white cribs, waiting? She can't picture it. She wishes she could feel the indignation that Nina feels, the sharp anger and suspicion that had made her want to do something, to make a stand. Jan knows what she should think —that both she and her mother are wrong, that the baby doesn't belong with either of them. But all she can concentrate on is the need pulsing throughout her, the lightning in her fingertips. She doesn't think her mother could understand it, that she could have ever felt this way.

Jan tries to picture the babies again, a big white room. It is impossible. She gives up. She stands there and thinks about when she was four or five years old instead. She can remember that, waking from a nap and just lying there, thinking about whether or not she should cry out. Waiting for someone to come. For something to happen.

dear john

WHEN MY HUSBAND first announced that he was leaving me, there were no packed bags. No studio apartment had already been leased on the other, seedier side of town. There were no missing photo albums or Le Creuset pots. But I don't know why he would have taken those things anyway. It would be a gradual process, he told me. He couldn't just up and leave me all at once, no matter how unhappy he was.

First it was his hands. Three days after he announced that he was going to leave me, I watched him drinking his coffee and noticed how his three middle fingers were slipped through the handle, gripping the body of the mug in a confident, almost loving way. I didn't recognize those strong fingers. Next it was his voice. You aren't going to leave me today, are you? I asked, turning to him in bed one morning three weeks after his announcement. Not today, he said. And his voice was not groggy and irritated and heavy with morning. It was rich and full, a voice I had never heard before. Next, flecks of brown and gold started to flash in his eyes. He would look at me, and those flecks were like little daggers of earnestness flaring out at me and waving hello from some new, secret place.

It has been months. Maybe years. He faces the shower head now, bold and unabashed in the strong spray. He is a very tall man now, with shoulders that stretch against the horizon. He eats steak and he exercises. We go to the movies and listen to music. A rich, olive tone has settled across his skin. His arms are strong and certain, no longer pale and wiry thin. When I smile, he smiles. Look at that little cat, he said the other morning. I joined him at the kitchen window and we watched the little cat slink across the street. We do that. We stand next to each other in the morning light and watch tiny, insignificant things happen right there in front of us.

He lost his scar today. The thin, almost invisible one across his left cheek from when we went sledding when we were very young. I had wanted to go fast. That was such a long time ago. He had pushed me so hard that he fell and hit his face against the runner of the sled. I had called it a love bite. Blood in the snow. He had only grimaced, his small hand hovering over the cut but not touching a thing.

In my mind, I secretly sort and catalog each way his body changes. The sudden, hard bulge beneath his shirtsleeves arrives on a Tuesday in October. The white teeth and the flexible toes in December, like Christmas. The vibrant ridge of his backbone. The happy earlobes. The kiss of flushed, healthy skin on the back of his neck. Sometimes I stare at him and convince myself that I can see him morphing right there in front of me. But then I blink, or look down at my plate, or fall asleep. And the next time I look at him, something else is brand new. More of him is gone.

My husband doesn't remember how we met. There's a look on his face when I quiz him—as if he knows it's not there, but he's going to dig through his mind regardless and show me that he's trying, that he knows how important this is.

My husband is a hearty lover. My husband is a good friend. He is a hearty, good man.

We had a baby once, I say. Nine and a half years ago. Maybe that's why I'm leaving, he says. Because of the baby. How long do you think she would have lived? I ask. If we had really had a baby girl? What name would you have given her? He looks at me with his beautiful, blank face. The strong plateau of his forehead does not scrunch or shift. I hate to say it, but it is almost enough when he places his big, flat hand over the top of mine. His hand is like a warm, tough palette of rising dough, and this is almost enough.

My husband used to have shoulders that sank when I laughed. Now his hair shimmers in the sunlight. I ask him if he got highlights. I ask him who he's trying to impress and tell him he doesn't look any younger. He just looks at me with his blank smile, his hair beautiful in the sunlight. When we hold hands he doesn't seem distracted. He has a new job. We have new friends.

My husband used to have moles. He had a few angry looking ones removed over the years. He used to worry. I tried to reassure him each time and tell him that it wasn't a big deal. It was just in case, that was all. He would mope around the house for days, sucked into the melodramatic daydream of his long, drawn out death. The drama was so tiresome. At night his ugly neediness would nestle in our bed like a solid, healthy baby, slumbering sweetly there between us. Now I try to trace all of the ghost places where little bits of him had been cut out by the dermatologist time and time again. I touch his perfect skin and wonder where they have gone off to—those shallow craters of shiny, stubborn tissue.

When my husband began to leave bit by bit, body part by body part, word by word, our dog didn't growl at him or sniff suspiciously. Not once.

When his laugh left—that hollow, sarcastic staircase of sound —I didn't mind. I don't miss the deep dimples above his knees. I don't miss the way he used to talk to me while brushing his teeth, gesticulating violently when I couldn't understand him. I don't miss his bony wrists. I don't miss the way he folded the laundry or how his wedding band bit into his finger. I don't miss his smile. I don't miss his nose. I don't miss his scent.

Where's John? I ask while we are out working in the garden. He looks at me long enough to simply shrug. The sun slants down and fingers his beautiful hair. His heavy work boot rests on top of the shovel blade. There is a long stretch of earth in our garden yet to be turned, and it vibrates with all of his magnificent, endless energy.

My husband used to make an entire pot of coffee in the morning, insisting that it was the only way to get the taste right. Now he makes four cups exactly and everything tastes fine. He tries to make up stories for me sometimes when we are in bed at night. He comes up with various tales about why he left, what mistakes the two of us might have made. There were fights, I tell him. I remember that, I say. We will be strangers together for the rest of our lives, trying to recreate a history even I have started to forget. He knows that I am sad. That I regret things now. That I miss him. I pretend to get excited at the thought of our retirement years stretched out before us like an empty, flat ocean.

Once, and this was many years ago, my husband wept after I surprised him and tickled him. Once upon a time, I used to enter a room and see him sitting alone at a table, his back to me.

Sometimes I stay stretched out in the bathtub after I've opened the drain so that I can feel the suck and pull of the disappearing water. When the bath water is gone, I rest my hands on the molded roundness of my hips. There was something he used to say. There was something he used to hint at. In a painting, I could be beautiful.

careless daughters

EACH TIME THEIR husband found them bunched up together on one of the couches, chuckling and chortling, or in the heavy swing out on the back porch doing the same, he'd laugh and look at them sideways and say, shyly, in his feathery voice: Hear my voice, ye careless daughters. Number three knew that this was a quote from the bible, but she couldn't remember exactly what part it came from or what it referred to. He said this often, even though he didn't believe in God. When he found them in a tight circle in the brightly-lit kitchen, or in a clump in the dank basement pulling tendrils of wet clothing out of the washing machine, he'd say it, and his three wives would chuckle. It didn't sound at all like a command when he said it. Hear my voice, ye careless daughters. It was a plea, his lips wet and his shoulders bunched up with joy and jubilation. He'd found his wives, all of them together somewhere within his home. And he loved the workings of his home.

She was number three. After she arrived, the three of them— number one, number two, and number three—became inseparable. They lived in his large house, which sat on several acres. The land had been farmland for over a century. Now it was a wide, green, empty set of lawns. A front lawn, a back lawn, two side lawns, all of it rolling and vast and useless. The three wives were jobless. This was his condition. They were in charge of the huge house, which always seemed to be clean and immaculate without much work or care from any one of them.

They spent almost all of their time together, sitting on the huge, soft couches or sprawled out on one of the wide lawns. Soon after number three arrived, she came to understand that these two women would become her best friends, no matter how strange the situation that she had gotten herself into became. She was no longer scared or uncertain. The man, her husband, seemed less large and less concrete when she saw number one and number two standing on either side of him. His harsher features began to melt like soft taffy once she became close with his first two wives. Somehow she'd made the right decision. Exactly the right one.

He mapped out their days and weeks on a sheet of butcher paper that covered the front of the refrigerator, giving each wife her own separate and solitary duties. It was a rigid schedule. But he didn't seem to mind when the three of them broke it and ended up spending most of the day together, lazily helping one another do their chores. He must have noticed the way their eyes glazed over and their expressions softened when they were together. Perhaps he didn't notice the birdlike hardness beneath all of that, their sharp, witty tongues and fast humor. To him, all three wives were tied together in a complicated way, a way that pleased him. He never seemed to recognize the singular fire between number one and number two.

The first thing number three saw when she drove into town was the Dairy Queen. It looked timeless, and she felt as if she were about to disappear. Part of her still did believe that she wouldn't go through with it. She would drive by the house slowly and stare and then she would leave this town and head home. There would be several more days of driving and motels, and then she'd be back in her bed again, afraid and in awe of what she had almost done. She wouldn't be able to tell anyone, even those who knew her well enough to believe it.

Number three was terrified when she first pulled into the long drive. It had been a lightheaded, ticklish kind of terror, lightly racing up and down her torso and finally belly flopping into her acid-filled stomach. Slowly dissolving there. When she walked in the front door, some of her things spilling out of her arms, she felt like she was the last guest to arrive for a sleepover. She saw number one and number two and she could sense the territorial claims that had already been made. She was late for the party.

Standing there, her big purse swinging heavily from her elbow and two of her bags clutched against her chest, she thought that she had finally discovered what it felt like to be alone. She imagined a tight force field surrounding her body, a glowing crust of pulsing light. No one can crack this, she thought. She was very sad, and almost happy. She glanced at number one and at number two and wanted to apologize for coming. They seemed older than her. They looked thin, fresh, and wise. She could never be one of them. She had this crusty, warm light buzzing around her, insistently telling her what it felt like to be all by your little old lonesome so damn assuming self.

After that split-second of standing there and feeling the force of the world and of loneliness, she was pulled in. They reached out their skinny arms and tugged at her, grabbing her things and dragging her further into the house. It was like lightning, this fast gesticulating and groping. The questions and the winking and the demonstrations of flight on the wide, polished banister. They were ravenous. And, like him, she never would have guessed during those first several weeks that they would ever, how could they, choose each other over her.

What's it like with him? number one asked one day while they were cleaning the wood floors. Number three stopped, a spray bottle of Old English holstered on her hip, her hand ready to grab and fire. You mean the sex? she asked. She had been there for two and a half weeks already and assumed that this was something the three of them did not discuss. The sex, the sex, the sex! Number two waved her arms in the air and shouted, almost slipping on the smooth, shining floor. This was their favorite chore to do together, and it was officially number three's job. Each of them stood on a pair of old rags and skid along the floors wherever she sprayed the Old English. They considered this their aerobic workout. Two thousand square feet of old, gleaming wood, every other day.

I'm not sure what to say, number three said, and then she sprayed a wide arc of Old English. The three of them skated after it.

It's a challenge, I think, number one said. She spun around and looked at number three. Her eyes were wide and clear, as if she expected number three to completely understand what she meant by that, a challenge. And so number three nodded.

Number one was a wise, bookish woman. She often read while the three of them lounged together after helping each other complete their chores. She read a haphazard variety of nonfiction books and knew how to do many things, most of which she hadn't ever done: how to garden in sandy soil; how to climb mountains; how to talk to the dead; how to knit blindfolded.

I think it's quite sad, number two said, her lips in a thin pout. Number two, an unsuccessful Broadway actress, loved to channel surf between two or three soap operas at a time, never fully grasping the storylines of any one program. She was dramatic, number three thought, and used the word "quite" too often, an affected habit that number three found outrageously annoying and brave.

Number three sprayed again and slid toward the falling mist of Old English, her mouth shut. She didn't know what to say about the sex. And so she pretended that it was a private affair and that she didn't wish to say anything about it. If she told the full truth, she'd have to admit that she thought about them while it was happening, not him. Nothing sexual. She would think about the two of them in the room at the end of the hall, each in her own full-sized bed. Reading, or channel surfing. And there number three was, in his huge and heavy bed, thinking about the two of them while he touched her in a way that was as familiar and as motivating as slipping on a pair of ordinary, just plain regular jeans.

Number one and number two skated in a tight circle around her while she thought about this. They watched her. She sprayed high, just over their heads, and they followed her as she pushed on through into the next wide room.

They had held a small, quiet ceremony in the living room a couple days after number three arrived, just the four of them. Number three wondered if any of it was legal. Her husband said that they would sign some papers eventually at the little court-house downtown. Number one and number two had stood next to her barefoot on the plush carpet, in nice, expensive-looking pantsuits. Number three realized that they were her bridesmaids. Her new husband did most of the talking. There weren't any set vows. He talked, in his quiet voice, about how pleased he was. The whole thing reminded number three of the long, drawling phone conversations that had taken place before they met in person. She had sat in her apartment, eating peanuts while they talked, thinking of the entire thing as a joke, an experiment. Cars were constantly honking, her windows rattling. He had asked lots of innocuous questions and had laughed quietly, like an old uncle she had forgotten about having. He sounded exactly the same that day in the living room. Only now she could see him: his little, squinty eyes and his immense belly. He was finally life-sized, not just a fluffy voice.

He said some things, and she nodded politely. Then there was a sudden, brief kiss. Their first one. Number three realized that she would be going to bed with this man that very night. She was neither curious nor repulsed. She was patient and tolerant, two things she'd never felt before. She felt soft and warm and accepting. She felt like shrugging her shoulders.

She jumped when she felt cold hands on the back of her neck. At first she thought that he was grabbing her, ready for another kiss, but fierce and passionate this time. If that was possible. Then she realized that number one and number two were pulling her back to them. They both had her neck in a claw-like grip. Before she turned around and faced them, number three thought that they were angry about the kiss, that she had already broken a complicated, unstated rule. Their fingers were quick and strong. She was relieved, filled with a mysterious pleasure, when she turned to them and saw that they were only pulling her in for hugs. Tight, insistent embraces that made the blood in her arms flow in entirely new directions.

The three of them erratically discussed their former lives and what they had left behind. Number three knew that number one had left her first husband and had come to the house six years ago with several crates of stolen library books that had been checked out under her first husband's name. Number two had arrived from New York City, penniless and fameless, two years after that. They shared general things about their pasts: favorite foods, biggest phobias, number of broken bones, etc. They mentioned specific people and events sporadically, never telling complete stories, but bringing up the names of certain people and places as if the three of them had known each other forever and there was no need for explanation. The omission of specific details and the lack of clarification seemed natural, even liberating. Number three's curiosity about the other wives' pasts began to fade after being with them for only about a week, along with her urge to talk about her own recently deserted life. As a secret game, she began to place number one and number two within her memories of events and moments that had occurred well before she had met them. They became the two older sisters she had never had. They had been there when she first began menstruating. They had held her hand and made her laugh after she had nearly choked on a cherry pit; she hadn't been home alone that afternoon at only six years old. When she was born, they had been there in the room. They had heard her first cry. And she had been a much better person for it. She had treated people, including herself, well.

Going out into town, number three realized, was like a mini-vacation. She would get excited before the three of them ran an errand. Her palms would start to sweat and she'd hide them in her pockets. She felt powerful when the three of them were out in public. At the grocery store, she'd notice people watching them. Especially women—in tight jeans, with poofy hair. There were plenty of rumors about the robust man in the huge house that sat at the southern edge of town. Plenty of people knew what he was up to, or were pretty good at guessing. Number two bought armloads of celebrity gossip magazines each time they went through the checkout lane. Number three imagined their faces on the front of one of the glossy covers, smiling hugely or looking away from the camera without a care in the world.

I bet you have a beautiful voice, number two said. It was late afternoon. The three of them were sitting on the steep stone steps that led up to the front door of the house. It was hot out, and they had been quiet for some time until number two said this, randomly, to number three. You've never heard me sing before, have you? number three asked. I've heard you hum, number two said, while doing things around the house. Number one leaned back on her elbows and said, So have I. There was the faintest of breezes, and she closed her eyes. I refuse to sing, number three said, standing. Number two swatted at her knees. Please? she whined. Something simple. I bet you'd sound Irish. I bet you have a reedy voice. Yeah, number one mumbled, her eyes still closed. There's nothing Irish in me, number three laughed. My voice is thick, like a frog's. She walked down the steps and sat in the grass, facing them. She hated her voice. She had mouthed the words when she was in the chorus of the seventh grade musical, terrified that someone would call her out on it. She wouldn't sing for them, but she loved that they wanted her to.

She watched them sprawled out on the stone steps, the huge house rising behind them like a beautifully detailed stage back-drop. She had never known that she could exist in a place like this, one too gigantic and extraordinary for the small, everyday town that it sat in.

Have we been brainwashed? Number one sat up suddenly. Are we insane? she asked. Even though she had opened her eyes, her face still had a dreamy, lost look. Are we? she asked, tilting her chin to the sun like a lethargic housecat. It's like an exclusive resort out here, number three said. Yeah, said number two, the middle of nowhere. Number one stretched her arms toward the sun. When we have a baby, she yawned, I wonder what room we'll put it in.

All three of them were quiet. Number three's heart jumped whenever one of them brought up talk of children. She wasn't excited about the idea of a child, exactly; she'd never thought that she would have a child until she moved here. She was excited about the three of them having something wild to do. They didn't often talk about becoming mothers. When they did, it felt like pretend. The other two wives had gone with number three to her first gynecological appointment in town. They teased her in the car on the way there, telling her how often they were sent in for tune-ups. The gynecologist—a short, plain woman—was quick and straightforward, just how number one and number two had described her.

The possibility of a child didn't feel real, but all three of them were vaguely curious about who would have one first. Deep down, number three assumed that it would simply work somehow. The child would belong to each one of them. They never discussed this, but they all knew that they would quit smoking, which they only did when they ran errands in the Volkswagen. It would be easy as pie, number three thought, squinting up at the house. She was filled with a heavy, hesitant sense of anticipation. Easy as pie. Before moving out here, she hadn't ever used phrases like that one. She hadn't ever felt this settled. This resigned.

There were a few solitary chores that each wife enjoyed doing on her own. Number one maintained the tiny, sad vegetable garden with a fastidious fury. She was protective of anything that managed to grow there and spent a couple hours after dinner each night out in the center of the large backyard, swatting at mosquitoes and pulling slugs off of her tomato plants. Number two was obsessed with changing the bed linens. She refused help from anyone, perfecting her meticulous folds, tucks, and creases alone. There were eight beds in the house. She changed the three beds that were used regularly every day. The other five beds were changed every other day, even though most of them hadn't been slept in by guests for months. Number three's private obsession became ironing. Number two was eager to hand the chore over to her after she arrived. She took number three down into the basement and showed her the corner of the utility room that housed an ironing board, an adjustable metal stool, and the most magnificent appliance number three had ever seen: the Triathlon Steamer, version 5.0. Just perfect for my little arms, number two said in her best soap opera voice, holding the large iron out to number three with both hands. She grimaced like an old stage actress until number three finally took the heavy iron into her own hands.

Most mornings the three of them, coffee cups in hand, wandered back and forth between the kitchen and the basement, adding fabric softener and unhurriedly transferring loads from the washer to the dryer. Once everything was dry and crisp and folded neatly into wicker baskets, number one and number two left number three alone to iron in the deepest corner of the utility room. A bare bulb illuminated her work. The ironing seemed archaic and romantic—all of the heat and steam filling the unfinished half of the basement, which number three began to think of as the heart of the massive house. The whole process made her want to stand up on the creaky metal stool and tap messages into the pipes that threaded the ceiling. The huge house felt extremely empty then. Three wives didn't seem to be nearly enough.

When number three had lived alone, she had never consciously separated her housework into specific chores. She had simply tried to keep her place clean. She swept the floors and did the dishes in a hurry, eager to be done. Her last lover had handwashed her curtains once and had enjoyed it, as if he were relishing a rare delicacy. While ironing, number three began to understand his pleasure in such an ordinary task.

Lately, when she looked into a mirror, number three saw that she was becoming more and more birdlike, similar to number one and number two. Her body was sharp and angular now. When she was alone, the Triathlon moving like silk over cotton, she tried to relax the tight, rubbery muscles in her shoulders and focus on the delicate softness that she used to notice in her cheeks and thighs.

A few months after number three arrived, on a night when it was her turn to sleep with their husband, the first wave of muffled cries reached her from the bedroom down the hall, just after the massive body beside her had fallen asleep. Before she heard the cries, she had been thinking about her husband, pressing her legs against his huge thigh. He slept. She had been thinking about how he had no children. How he seemed both sexual and sexless at the same time, impotent and happy. Gently and humbly androgynous, even during sex. Likeable. When she moved away from him and shifted onto her back, number three heard the cries. They sounded like soft, muffled things by the time they reached her from the opposite end of the hall, working their way through two sets of closed doors. But she knew what they were. Cries of passion. Whimpers of release. Groans of rapture. Glorious, magnificent, splendid love sounds.

Sex sounds. Sounds she never made with him.

Number three lay there, paralyzed. Slowly, she realized that when she was alone ironing each day, number one and number two were off somewhere making similar sounds, which couldn't reach her in the deepest corner of the basement. They left her down there—surrounded by baskets of barely wrinkled clothing, amid pillows of steam, wielding a concentrated point of heat—and found each other in vacant rooms, some of which were just above the rising vapor of her most precious work. The cries pulled everything together: a pair of hands lingering on a bowl; a glance that she wasn't, she now realized, supposed to see.

Number three couldn't say that she was surprised when she discovered the secret relationship that existed between number one and number two. Their life was strange and isolated. The three of them constantly crammed themselves together, sharing a long list of subtle intimacies that most girlfriends never know. Lounging together, cooking together, washing the tall windows together, they learned things about each other's bodies and minds. Number three liked to imagine that something passed through them during all of the time that they spent so close together—something like a light, filmy mist. It slipped from one woman to the next, changing them, randomly exchanging pieces of them. This was something that none of them, of course, could physically feel.

If number three wasn't surprised, she was angry. She couldn't imagine being intimate with either woman. She felt like a school girl again, irrational and explosive. Dangerous. She felt worked up and tight, like when she used to walk into the living room and stare at her mother, who just sat there on the couch, her jaws popping while she worked at her chewing gum. Her mother was always fixing something, socks with holes in the heels or wicker laundry baskets that had come unwoven. Her fingers were always working, her jaws always snapping. Number three would grow angry if she stood there and watched her mother for long enough. Sometimes she'd yell and say something mean, or even shove her mother hard in the shoulder if she wasn't listening.

That familiar tightness wound itself up inside of number three. Any feelings that could have become shock or grief or understanding were stunted and expertly shaped into rage. To number three's amazement, however, the rage stayed within her rib cage, pulsing and ricocheting. She kept it there deftly, to herself, and continued to treat the other two wives as if there were tenderness flying in her chest. Not fury.

She paid more attention to her husband. She wondered what it was, exactly, that she felt for the man. Sometimes she found herself pretending that she was his only wife. She wondered what conversations they might have each day. She wondered if he would look at her differently if she were the only one. One night after dinner, when number one was off in her garden and number two was upstairs flipping through the hundreds of cable channels, number three's husband told her that he had seen a three-legged deer on the way to work that morning. Just walking along the side of the road, he said, shrugging. Even though he didn't seem at all stunned by this sighting—a three-legged deer!—number three hoped that he didn't think enough of the event to tell the others. Perhaps that story, the deer, could belong to just the two of them. Number three felt dizzy when she thought this. She felt compassionate and caged.

Her husband was often a hard man to read. His small eyes never widened. They were always squinty and dry, a pair of tiny windows with the dark, stale shades drawn tight. She had to guess what he thought and felt, unless he was extremely happy and pleased; his shoulders would bunch up then. And so she blindly pretended, from time to time, that she was his only wife. This pretending was difficult, especially when it was her turn to share his bed. Number three couldn't avoid trying to guess which of the two full-sized beds in the bedroom down the hall was abandoned. She pictured the vacant bed, the empty expanse of tightly made sheets suffocated by a large goose down comforter. Focusing on the empty bed was her attempt—a faltering one—not to imagine the rustling and the turning that was taking place in the identical bed right next to it.

At a barbeque with some of her husband's friends, all of whom had multiple wives themselves and were from nearby cities and towns, number three stuck by his side. She pressed herself into him and held his arm, weaving with him through the small crowd of men—all of them soft, like him, and blandly tender. The fire on the barbeque was hot and well controlled. There was low laughter. She got her husband a beer. Her head began to hurt from trying to feel like the lone, spectacular wife.

She turned, finally, and focused on the shrill swarm of wives off by the badminton net. The mass of women was compressed and alive, full of fluttering limbs and delighted, jerking necks. Most of the wives had bodies similar to number three's. She had gotten used to the new, hard image in the mirror. The gauntness and the firm muscle made sense. When she and the other two wives were together they moved quickly, even while relaxing. They laughed sharply and grabbed at various things and at each other. When they rested on the huge, soft couches, they seemed to pant while lying there, some mysterious parts of their bodies still working double and triple time.

Number two came over and pulled number three away from their husband. She bent close to number three's face. Her breath smelled like acidic fruit and gin. She laughed in number three's ear and whispered, dramatically, We're discussing shoplifting. She sighed wetly onto number three's earlobe. Have you ever done it? she asked. When you were especially young?

There was the secret rage fluttering in number three's chest, the sting of betrayal. But there was also loneliness, a new kind that she hadn't discovered until now. Number two pulled her into the snug flock of wives, and number one grabbed her hand when she saw her, pulling her in even further. The entire crowd of women smelled like fruit and gin. Someone offered her a cool glass of something that tasted exactly like the smell. She drank and stood in between number one and number two. Even though everyone in the group was smiling and sharing secrets, she felt as if the other two wives were protecting her from something. They stood straight and rigid on either side of her, quietly watching her while she drank. The attitude and intensity within the circle of women was not unfamiliar. The three of them acted this way all the time, talking in loud, fearless voices and nodding at each other ecstatically. But on such a large scale, with so many women involved, the experience was a bit frightening and grotesque to number three. She knew that the other two wives could sense her discomfort. Surely they both remembered their own first experience within a large, flashy crowd of multiple wives, all of the teeth and the fingers and the crawling laughter.

Number three's anger, spurred on by her extreme discomfort, reared up for a quick moment, hesitant to strike. Then it fell back, softly, against her heart. She looked at the two women on either side of her. Number one's thick plait of hair barely moved in the breeze. Number two's gentle, pale hands opened and closed at her sides. Nothing could be done, number three decided, to make them stay.

The Triathlon Steamer, version 5.0, had a soft, ergonomic handle. It had a scratch-resistant, stainless-steel laser soleplate with a precision tip. Number three read the owner's manual and memorized the beautiful terminology. Thirty-one microholes and eighteen-hundred watts. A twenty-five percent larger water tank than the previous models for more board time and less fill-ups. The iron felt heavy but well-balanced in her hand. She relished pulling the steam trigger and filling the room with haze.

Number three began to iron everything: towels, socks, cleaning rags. She'd hole herself up in the deep corner of the utility room and stay there for hours. Eventually number one and number two stopped coming down to get her, looks of genuine concern creasing the smooth skin between their neat eyebrows. They let her be for entire afternoons. And she wouldn't think about them. She wouldn't try to guess what they might be doing at any given moment, together. She slid the hot iron over anything that was made of cloth. She experimented wildly with various settings. She kept her eyes on the ironing board and ignored the clouds of rising steam, which dissolved against the pipes and the ceiling, sometimes just below number one and number two.

On the day that they left, it took number three quite a while to realize that they were gone. She was holding the iron, about to turn it off. She was surrounded by baskets of hot, folded clothing. She looked up at the ceiling, closed her eyes, and realized.

⌒

NUMBER three's sleep is restless and intermittent. She wakes up and stares into the blackness of the room, refusing to look at the alarm clock. She can tell that he is asleep. The quiet in the bedroom has changed. It is crisp and piercing. She's the only one listening to it now. He's gone, his hands folded and riding high on top of his round belly as he breathes in and out, deeply. She tries to listen for any sounds outside of the bedroom. She waits for little cries, screams of delight, sighs of ecstasy to wash down the long hall and slide underneath the door, then touch her. The emptiness of the house feels tingly against her skin, like a membranous shell delicately looped through with arteries and fingers of nerves. She presses into him while he sleeps. It feels as if they are at the center of everything, of emptiness.

It was supposed to be number one's turn with their husband tonight. Number three had entered his bed cautiously, as if she were trespassing. She had waited for a steel trap to bite into her leg, an alarm to sound. There was nothing.

It is the first night that number one and number two have been gone, and their husband had seemed resigned to the fact that they were gone for good before he fell asleep. He had held number three's hand. He had seemed sad and rundown, yet oddly economical. I'll have to put out another ad, he had said. And he asked number three to write it for him. According to the placement company that he uses, ads written by current wives receive the most responses from single women. Ads written by men are 'me, me, me,' he explained to number three drowsily. Not welcoming and sincere like the ones written by women.

Number three lies in the dark and thinks about the ad that she herself had answered, the short, enthusiastic message that had brought her across the country and into a stranger's home. Number one and number two must have sat down together and written it. Number three tries to remember exactly what the ad she had stumbled across on the internet had said. She had been bored at work when she found the website, fascinated by the idea of a man offering her a free, comfortable life. She can't think of the specific words that were used.

Lying there next to the immenseness of her husband's sleeping body, number three considers his request. He had asked her to write the ad in such a simple and straightforward manner, as if he completely expected her to comply. Now she can feel the anger creeping out of the snug place where she's been hoarding it ever since she found out about number one and number two. She wants to laugh; there's no more holding it in. Her lips quiver. Before she had left everything and moved out here, her anger used to be sharp, immediate, and strong. She hadn't ever held it in. She had honked her car horn a lot. She had yelled at the TV when the news upset her. She had let her best friend and college roommate sleep outside on the stoop when she forgot her key to the apartment for the fourth time. She had yelled through the door and called her a no-good drunk.

The sudden pulse in number three's temple is familiar. It is a steady drumming that, at last, lulls her into an unbroken sleep. Four nights later, number three has a dream in which she is the mother of a child. In her dream she is at a gas station. The child is a tiny, bald infant, and it talks with her sensibly while she pumps gas into a car that she has never seen before. It is early morning when she wakes up. Number three lies in bed and tries to remember what the baby had said to her. She can't recall a single word. When her husband stirs beside her, number three inexplicably clutches her chest. She gasps at what she feels—two hard, large lumps. One in each breast.

Again, the gynecologist works quickly and bluntly. She presses number three's breasts firmly and probes the contours of the lumps with stiff, cold fingers. That's liquid in there, she says, wielding a long needle attached to a hollow plastic tube. I'm going to have to aspirate those lumps, she says, to see exactly what's in there. Number three does not like the word "aspirate." Suddenly the gynecologist is hovering over her, and the needle has slipped neatly into her left breast.

The gynecologist fills three little paper cups with breast milk. She asks number three if she could be pregnant. Number three says that she doubts it. Somehow she is certain of this. The gynecologist tells her to go to the drugstore and buy a couple of at home pregnancy tests anyway, just to be certain. She offers to do a blood test, but the results would take a couple days. I've heard of this happening, the gynecologist says dryly. But of course it's rare. She sighs. You're just desperate for a child, and you've convinced your body that one is inside of you. Our bodies do strange things, she says before leaving number three alone to get dressed. Number three stares at the breast milk. She imagines that she can smell it, a sickly sweetness in the air. She can't think of the breast milk as her own. She tries to tell herself that she wants the child from her dream, that she's desperate. She tries, but she can't even remember its facial features, or the sound of its voice.

She takes two pregnancy tests at home. Both are negative. Number three waits for a reaction to rise within her—thudding relief or simple grief. Instead it's the anger, which still feels somewhat distant and imprecise. There is no single whiplash of fury, and this makes her restless. She paces the kitchen and then decides to finally write the ad. The day after number one and number two had left, her husband had printed off a list of ad-writing tips from the placement company's website and stuck it onto the front of the fridge, right in the middle of his butcher paper chart of chores. He's been waiting patiently ever since. Number three scans the ad-writing tips for the first time. Follow the five W's— who, what, when, where, and why/how. Don't include body part requirements or sexual preferences. Don't write in all-caps; this screams at the reader. Avoid "gibber" that says nothing. For example, "U R Cute." A phrase at the end of the list catches number three's eye: "the elusive sisterwife." She imagines number one and number two as one person, a monstrous woman with two furious heads. Her sister. Her wife.

Once when it had been number two's night with their husband, number one had said number three's name softly, just before falling asleep. There was no "goodnight," only the weight of her name shifting lightly between the two full-sized beds. What would have happened if number three had been the one to arrive second? For the first time, she tries to imagine where the other two might be. She tries to imagine a bewildered look on their faces, the two of them sitting in a shadowy corner, missing her. There won't be any letters or e-mails, number three decides. They won't contact her. They have completely cut her off and abandoned her. This wasn't a permanent life for us, they seem to be telling her, laughing in her face. She feels stuck here, now that she thinks about it, her legs trapped in thick mud, which is reaching up just past her kneecaps and hardening there.

Number three sits down at the kitchen table with a pad of paper and a pencil. She can't think of how to begin. Her mind wanders and she thinks of the few things that she gave away before moving here. She writes a short list, an incomplete inventory. Her potted ferns. An antique paperweight she gave someone at work. She wants these things back. She could write a letter demanding that they be returned to her.

Instead, number three tears up her list and glances at the refrigerator, trying to wade through the formula of ad-writing tips. She makes herself start. She says that she is seeking the elusive sisterwife. She says that she likes to bake and to shop on-line. She lies and says that she sings. She says that her husband has a great sense of humor and that the house is charming. As soon as she writes these things down she attacks them, crossing out words and adding dark, cutting commas. Her sentences fall apart.

The smell of burning leaves sifts in through the open kitchen window. This scent startles number three. She considers the smell of smoldering leaves to be a farm smell, and this property has not been a farm for decades. The scent must have blown over from a few miles away, a ghost smell on a dead farm. She rises and looks out the window. Her husband is standing far out in the back lawn. The sight of him standing there is a shock; he's never home during the day. Number three goes out the backdoor and walks toward him. The sharp pinches from the needle return to her chest. She walks slowly, deciding that she wants a family with this man. Isn't that why she came here? She lets this become the reason. She decides that this is why she didn't confront number one and number two. The muted heat of fury in her chest has become familiar. She tells herself that she can use it for something. She'll be a mother.

The sky is wide and open. He stands against it, unaware of her approach. Wisps of his unkempt hair abandon themselves to the breeze. His face is raised to the sun. His legs are firmly planted. She can't see the bulge of his gut, but she knows that it's there, gracefully falling over the tight wall of his belt. Her father used to lift her over the neighbors' fence and drop her, carelessly, into their yard. Go play, he'd say, without knowing if the little girl who was about her age was even home. There are no fences here. She could just keep walking, it seems.

Number three tells him about the pregnancy tests as soon as he turns and sees her. She hadn't known that she was going to tell him. They were both negative, she says. He watches her. The dry, tight bulbs that are his eyes tell her nothing. I've started the ad, she says, suddenly certain that someday soon this man will impregnate her. She forces this certainty into her belly, stubbornly holding it down until it stops squirming. The ad isn't important. Maybe he won't even post another one, she thinks. Standing there against the green of the lawn and the blue of the sky, he looks small and infertile. Number three tells herself that she could somehow be enough for him.

We should shoot for a single mom, he says. We could really help someone like that out. He blinks at her. And her womb, the place where she imagines that she would carry a child, punches her from the inside.

What are you doing here? she asks, trying to sound casual. I took the rest of the day off, he says. I've been missing them. His voice is dramatic when he says this, a bad impression of number two's. He turns and faces the sun again. He says, I'm glad that you started the ad. The smell of burning leaves is stronger now, thick. Number three inhales and says, I'm your wife. He nods. His neck is a thin, pale stalk. There is a crisp snap within her. The wound-up tightness in her body loosens. Finally, there is a rush. I'm your wife! she screams into the open space of the yard. She rushes forward and pushes him as hard as she can. He gasps, but his feet remain planted. I'm your wife! she screams again, pushing at him. She says, We'll have a child, the two of us. She pushes him again, hitting hard. He won't touch her. He won't even try to swat her away. Her hands bounce off of his solid belly. She won't give up. She charges, holding her thin, pointed shoulder out like a sharp javelin.

He is caught off guard when he falls. She can tell by the way his shoulders bunch up next to his small ears. He lands flat on his back. She sits on top of him, crying. She shifts her bony weight into his stomach, poking around. She wants to see him naked, lying there with nothing to protect him. She wants to see the parts of his body that she only feels in the dark. But he lies there fully clothed, his small eyes watching her. She can't tell if he's alarmed, or sad, or amused, or angry. His eyes won't say a thing. He is still, and she stares at him.

He's no longer impotent beneath that open sky. His body is soft and waiting. He is certain of what he'll have someday. It's our hardness, number three thinks, picturing herself lounging on one of the couches with number one and number two. Even though they would have taken care of any baby with a fierceness, nothing could grow in the sudden angles and hard lines of their bodies. And maybe that's why they left, she thinks. Because nothing ever grew.

There had been the child at the gas station, the bald, blank-faced infant that had talked to number three in her dream with a pleasant sense of urgency. That child was ours, she decides, rolling off of her husband's stomach and lying beside him in the grass. She says it aloud, testing the way it sounds. That child was ours. She can hear her husband's breathing change, becoming more rapid. She knows that he's about to pull himself up onto his elbows and look down at her. She'll see his bland, crinkled face staring at her from the open sky. Ours? he'll ask. What do you mean? What child?

She waits, listening to him breathe. Late afternoon passes. Shadows begin to yawn and stretch, and still her husband does not rise. Number three falls into the arrhythmic dance of his breathing. Some of their breaths are sharp, and some are soft.

Something impossible might be about to happen, number three thinks, breathing along with him. He might have a heart attack and die right here in the back lawn. Or he might pull me to him and fumble with my clothes, not caring that we are outside, that we can see each other.

Whatever does happen, she knows that she'll see his face first, above her, staring down from that sky. And so she decides.

It's alright if I just close my eyes.

produce

I'VE STARTED GROCERY shopping at one of the new, big places that takes up an entire city block, but claims to support the environment and our health and world peace and all of that. It's one of those multi-billion-dollar chains that claims to be making a difference in the world, but you still feel just as lost in the glare of the floors as you would in any other grocery store. I can barely afford to walk away with half a bag of groceries each week, but it's a habit I can't break. I go there for the produce. They've got a woman there who cries over all of the produce—row upon row upon row of all the organic stuff that they ship in from across the world (and perhaps the galaxy). African Butternut Magpie Berry Fruits. Japanese Dancing Mudpie Banana Nuts. Okay. So maybe I'm making those particular names up, but the names are outrageous all the same. And this woman that's been hired to cry over all of this crazy expensive produce wears one of the stiff-collared shirts with the tight company logo stitched right above the heart. She seems pretty efficient, scurrying from row to row.

She cups her hands beneath her eyes when she's walking from one display to the next so that she doesn't waste any of her tears. She lets them fall gently between her fingers and rain down onto the butter lettuce and the red kale. I've never seen a single tear end up on the gleaming floor. I guess someone could slip and fall and sue the place if that happened. And I bet it hasn't, because why would she still be working there? She cries. And each of us has our own little modern looking cart with smooth, silent wheels. We move around each other silently. But she's always making noise, the woman who cries on the produce. Usually it's just soft, little sounds. Lots of sighs. You get the sense that there's some kind of melancholy and longing in her heart (just below the store's logo) for something distant. Maybe something that she's forgotten about in a way. But then there are days when I shop there and she is standing over the flawless tomatillos or the crisp sea beans just wailing and letting out gut-wrenching sobs and little shrieks and screams. On those days, she's crying about something specific and raw and very real. We all push our silent carts and pretend not to notice. We brush by her shuddering shoulders in order to get to the choicest kumquat, the most perfect star fruit. Those are the best days. I swear you can see the stuff growing more beautiful right before your eyes. Firmer or softer. Plumper or tighter. I have to fight the urge to fill my cart to the brim on those days. I make my choices and then I head toward the checkout area as slowly as possible. I hate to rush it. Sometimes I browse new, expensive products that I'll never buy or understand. I take my time scoping out the free samples. And then I look for the longest checkout line. But, oh, the feeling. The cloth handles of my designer shopping bag (no plastic in that place, of course) press into the crook of my arm during the long walk home, leaving behind a woven indentation that I wish would never fade away. When I get back to my apartment, I take my time. I really do try to. I put things away. I wipe down the counter, even though it is already clean. I sharpen the sharp knife. If I could, I would press pause on the entire world before slicing into it. But I can't. I slice into it, then, when there is nothing else to do. The magnificent glistening there. The deep, sweet smell before you even see it or touch it or taste it. The very center of her grief.

my husband's house

> Down at the bottom of that dirty ol' river
> Down where the reeds and the catfish play
> There lies a dream as soft as the water
> There lies a bluebird that's flown away
>
> —*Townes Van Zandt, "Catfish Song"*

I DIDN'T GO looking for my husband's new place until after his fourth or fifth late night visit, after a long day when the sun had set without much color. I couldn't believe what he had told me that first time he showed up in the middle of the night in our bedroom a few weeks after he had gone missing, a living ghost. Yet the first place I tried was the river. The further you follow the river back into the woods, the further back in time you go. Kirk's favorite noodling spot is beneath an old railroad bridge that must be at least eighty years old, a bunch of broken timbers running across the water. When I got there that night, the water was slow and not too cold. It came up to my thighs when I reached Kirk's spot nestled into the far bank.

I stood in the dark water, my feet shifting in the silt, and continued to not believe my husband. I crouched down—the water pulling at my old blouse, seeping up its seams—and cursed him for telling lies. Reaching with my right hand, I closed my eyes and felt my chin hit the water. I didn't believe him. But I'd been drinking, and that was enough to make me curious. It was enough to let me change my mind once everything started to happen, the tugs and the pulls and the sinking shift. I was relieved and tired when I realized that my husband had been telling the truth, that there was no way to stop what was happening. I could feel it then: all of Ohio, its towns and its churches and its roads and its rivers—this old, snaky one especially—swallowing me up.

It makes you feel like singing, like burping after a fine meal and then closing your eyes, because who cares if anyone heard.

THE day when I first saw my husband was fine enough. The sky was clear with only a few, scattered clouds. And my father was smiling.

I had promised him that I would go fishing for the first time in a very long time. Too long. He was getting old and gray and soft-tempered. But he was quick and more alive on that particular day as we trudged down to the washed-out, foamy bank with our tackle and our long, awkward poles. The sun was bright. There was no need to talk about anything. He kept his promise and didn't smoke a single cigarette. But he did fumble plenty with his stiff shirt pocket, looking away with a guilty grimace.

When we reached the shore we saw two heads floating just above the surface of the water a few feet out. The day felt less wonderful.

"He won't come out," one of the men shouted, looking right at us, his head bobbing. He looked to be about my father's age, white eyebrows frowning above sunken eyes. The other man, who was much younger, grunted and bobbed, working at something a couple feet below the surface. He seemed to be tying a complicated knot without looking. The older man watched him closely, as if he were ready to either pull him toward shore or dunk him and hold him beneath the surface in an instant.

"Are they drunk?" I asked, expecting my father to be just as baffled.

"That's noodling, Nessa," my father said.

I looked at him. His smile had taken over his entire face, including his eyes and the crease in his forehead. My father's smile from just a few moments before had been dead compared to this one.

I watched the younger man and realized that he was fighting something beneath the surface. He was tugging at it, and it was viciously pulling back. He was in pain, but he hid it well beneath the quiet shell of his face. I could see the excitement coloring his high cheeks and the top of his throat. He was handsome.

I had grown up hearing plenty of stories about the noodling that occurred on the outskirts of my town, just off the sparsely wooded shores of the river. I knew it was illegal. I knew it sometimes took place during picnics, after a long day of drinking. I knew that men worked in pairs. They took off their shirts and waded into murky water, reaching into hollow logs, abandoned steel drums, and smooth dugouts in the muddy banks, waiting for the bite and pull of a nesting male catfish that could be decades old and weigh eighty-five pounds if you were lucky. When I was growing up, my father told me that these men, many of whom he worked with in construction, were crazy, barely holding onto a dying tradition. But I knew that my father was interested, that he was envious. I didn't understand why he would have no part of their secret club. He tried to scare me. He told me stories about giant cats pulling children off of riverbanks and eating them whole. I loved how my father's simple, no-fuss details could frighten me. Nameless, blank-faced children got too close to the water's edge. They were swallowed up. The end.

The two strangers now had stern looks on their faces. The younger one's shoulder muscles rolled smoothly as he reached deeper into the brown water, his chin dipping below the surface. Seeing someone noodle for the first time, after so many years of wondering and imagining, was like seeing a fairytale come true. I was uncomfortable standing there on the flimsy bank. I didn't like how complicated fairy tales could become. All the colors of the day began to change. The younger man's black, thick hair somehow shimmered like copper. There were blues and greens and even purples shining on the dead-flat surface of the water. There was brightness where brightness shouldn't be when you're looking out at a scrawny, dirty, over-fished river. I wanted to look away and stare at things that I knew would still be dull and dirt-covered: my old tennis shoes, the ancient tackle box that hadn't been pulled out of my father's basement for months.

I had no idea how big the cat was, just that it was fighting back with everything it had. The older man calmly watched the wrestling match and then, when his partner's head disappeared beneath the surface, he grabbed him by the ankles and would not let go.

I held my breath when the younger one went under. The musky scent of the river disappeared. I knew he would look puny when he came up, river water dripping from his ears and the tip of his nose. When he finally pulled himself up onto the shore and dried off and got dressed, he would be any other adult man from this part of town. Faded corduroy work pants, broken shoe-laces, an everyday voice, a hard, sweaty job.

When he didn't come up for air, I started to breathe again. I could feel our entire town resting on top of him, open fields and shallow valleys reaching boldly into Kentucky, growing deeper there. He surfaced with a smile on his face. He looked right at me, ignoring the gigantic cat that he had in a fierce bear hug. He didn't pay any attention to the whip-like whiskers or the large waves created by the submerged tail, stirring up the stink of the river. I expected a fish that big to have huge eyes, like hardboiled eggs. Instead they were little, black, and beady, encased in a thin film of blindness that reminded me of the empty stare of a puppet. The fish's head was wide and flat, with mammoth lips. The backbone seemed desperate to break through dull green rubber skin.

I know it all sounds too easy, but I considered falling in love with my husband that late-summer day because the noodling season was dying and wouldn't be back for another year. I considered it when I found out that he was also spending the day with his father. The coincidence was too hard to ignore, no matter how ordinary or trivial it was.

"I'll keep this one," my husband said, letting the cat fight in his arms until there wasn't any fight left. It took forever. I stood there patiently, watching all of that fight slip away and disappear like the last gust of a funnel cloud just before it dies. It was that good. It was just that sad.

Kirk first got physical with me when I dropped the car keys in the 7-Eleven parking lot. He pushed me from behind while I was stooped over and then grabbed my arm to stop me from toppling onto the pavement. He squeezed my arm as hard as he could until we got to the car. It started with stupid, random things like that. Things I couldn't predict. I'd be washing dishes at the sink and he'd pull my right arm hard behind my back, nuzzle into my neck and squeeze my wet wrist until my fingertips went white. From that very first incident in the parking lot I figured that if I stayed quiet and still, he'd loosen up and his eyes would clear. It was an instinct I had. We didn't have all-out fights. Kirk didn't shout and fling me against the wall. He didn't hit me. Instead there were these odd, quiet moments of holding on too hard, always a surprise. A hard pinch above my ribs when I got out of the bathtub. My thigh between his legs just before we fell asleep; he squeezed and squeezed until I had a purple halo of tenderness on my upper leg the next morning. This didn't start until after Kirk's father passed away, and then mine. Kirk's father died of a stroke before we were even engaged. Mine had a heart attack just days after the wedding and died a week later. I blame the way Kirk and I got started on all that grief.

Walt, Kirk's best friend and noodling partner, once told me that Kirk was like a dancer when they were in the water together. "He knows exactly when to move," Walt said. "Like it's all been planned out." Walt's wife, Jean, and I spent many Saturdays on the bank of the river watching our husbands noodle, a Styrofoam cooler of beer between us. We hardly talked to each other at all back then. We kept our hard stares on our husbands and held on tight to those cans of beer. And when we got drunk enough, watching the two of them work together in the muddy water was like watching what I imagine something like a water ballet must look like. Each man seemed to know exactly how long the other was going to be under. When one of them surfaced, the other already had a hold of the cat's tail. They pulled it ashore together. I guess when Kirk grabbed onto me and clenched too tightly, it was our own sort of dance. The pain—those nagging pinches, my wrists burning—didn't matter.

When I moved in with Kirk, I was informally inducted into our town's secret ring of noodlers. They are protective men, cagey and proud of what they do. But they didn't seem to care when I overheard their careful talk of how to elude game wardens or how to tend an arm that's been half skinned by sandpaper lips. There had been wives in the past who had been brave and romantic enough to serve as their husbands' noodling partners. I'd have no part of it. I was afraid of reaching into a cat hole and discovering a snapping turtle or an angry muskrat. I was still wary of my father's stories about children being yanked off the shore.

Kirk convinced me to wade into the water with him only once, not too long after his father had passed away. Anger settles on him so much easier than grief, like the finest river silt, and I was afraid to say no to him that day. He took me to one of his luckiest spots, a wooded shore where a section of an old highway overpass had collapsed who knows how long ago. I was excited when he said he felt something. "Knock, knock," he said. "Someone's home." He stuttered slightly, and I realized that he was afraid. Noodling without your partner is too risky. I looked down at my husband's skinny legs. For a moment, I felt like reaching into that dusky water and feeling what he felt. But then he was under and that cat had an immediate, unforgiving hold on his arm. The fish spun, twisting Kirk's shoulder so badly that I could hear him scream underwater. I stood there, too shocked to move. When Kirk finally came up without the catfish, blood trickling down from his elbow, I thought he was going to twist one of my arms back behind me or grab my shoulder or neck. "Damn," was all he said, a surprised whisper.

I didn't get in the water with him again after that. But I did learn how to skin and gut a giant cat. We'd hang it from a rope that Kirk had slung around the thickest branch of the old maple in our front yard, the hard row of gills caught on a heavy, iron hook. I quickly learned how to avoid drawing my own blood after the first and only time I stuck myself in the wrist with one of the spiny ventral fins. I learned how to pull the skin off in large, smooth sheets with a pair of pliers. I knew how to cut a neat slit along the fat belly, from the gills down to the anus. I reached in and pulled everything out, burying the guts later near the vegetable garden out back. Sweating and panting, with my hands and arms searching deep inside the carcass of a giant cat, I always expected to find something fantastic. An outboard motor, a dead dog, a sleeping baby. I'd shiver when my fingertips grazed something and then I'd pull it out and see it. A couple of empty mussel shells, a rounded river stone, a faded Coca-Cola can.

I can cook up a mean flathead. I used to serve it fried with cayenne pepper. During noodling season, my husband's buddies would bring me their catches, fillets as long as my leg that I would have to chop up into several thick steaks. I would listen to them talk while I cooked, sometimes for hours, that white, sweet, pecan-tasting meat hanging over the edges of my largest skillet. I took mental notes for my dead father. I was hearing everything. Somehow, I knew he would be pleased.

Walter told the best stories. My favorite was about how once, after a long Fourth of July day of drinking, he found himself alone in the river, wading from mud bank to mud bank. He spotted a cat hole and, partner-less, reached in. He said that he didn't remember the fight. He just remembered pulling himself onto the bank afterward and seeing that both of his arms were cut up and bleeding. The blood made him so angry that he went right back into the river and reached in again. He said that it was like a dream. He pulled that cat onto the shore and made it dance. When Walt told his stories, he'd be drunk and smiling. I swear that I could smell him from across the kitchen: a light, cedary scent slipping beneath the filmy aroma of fried catfish.

Walt's wife, Jean, would be there on those nights, the only other woman. She'd make cornbread or just sit there on a stool next to the stove, silently keeping me company while I cooked. Jean is a delicate woman, something I don't think I could ever be. Even her tongue is delicate, rarely showing itself, pink and small, the tip perfectly pointed and round. During Walt's stories, with Jean sitting right there next to me, I'd imagine being his wife. I'd listen to his voice, the softest voice of any man I know, and watch him gesture with his massive hands. Walt first cheated on Jean early in their marriage. We all knew about it. The two of them had been barely twenty years old at the time, immature and mean because they didn't know each other yet. Jean never talked about it with me. She and Walt had the best marriage out of any of us. There were rumors of Walt still wandering from time to time, stories that we all knew were as true as the day is long.

There was too much drinking on those nights. I'd pour cold beer onto the frying fillet and watch it spit. By the end of the night, Kirk would become agitated about any little thing. He would get short with Walter. He would call me Vanessa instead of Nessa, rolling his eyes if I said anything. He would grab my wrist and jerk it hard in front of the guys, as if he were getting ready to do even more while they were sitting right there. But that's not what I try to remember about those nights. I remember the skinny length of Kirk pressed next to me in bed after the others had left, the satisfying stink of catfish coming at us in waves from the small kitchen. All through the spring and up to the end of summer, we'd crawl into bed drunk and tired like that. He'd have to get up in just a few hours for another day of construction work. I'd have to drag myself to the cramped, musty daycare where I'm assistant manager. But we could lie there next to one another and be happy and alive for a while. Sleep doesn't matter when you are feeling that way.

I understand now that my father wanted me to get out of this town somehow. Maybe that's what his stories about monster catfish were for when I was a little girl. But there was a funny falling feeling in the center of my chest at the end of those catfish nights, a sensation I couldn't ignore. After a long day of working with other people's ragged, tired children and then a long night of skinning and cooking and listening, I'd relish the hard ache in my limbs, that sinking center in my chest while dawn teased the corners of my eyes. And if anyone had said anything to me about leaving then, I wouldn't have been able to imagine living any other kind of life in any other kind of town.

When Kirk disappeared, Walt had turned his back for a moment to watch the Canada geese that were flying low above the opposite bank. Kirk had been feeling out his favorite spot. "Someone can't drown and disappear like that," Walt said to me later that night, shaking and suddenly small. "Not while I'm just staring at birds." After fifteen days, they gave up trying to find Kirk's body. The river was shallow and the reeds were thin. There was nowhere else to look. Jean started passing evenings with me at my place. But I wanted her husband, Walt. That's what I have to admit. I wanted him when I was especially tired, the night insects bumping up against the screens like that.

The first time Kirk came back to me, after he had been missing for nearly four weeks, he woke me just past midnight. He was crouched above me, his lips above my left cheek. And the first thing I felt wasn't relief or joy or confusion. I felt guilty about the way he had found me stretched out across the mattress, my legs reaching into the emptiness of his side of the bed.

"I can't stay the night," was the very first thing he said. There was sorrow in his voice, but also a shade of power and delight. "I've got my own place now," he said. "That's where I've been, and where I'll be staying from now on."

I didn't argue with him. I was more scared of him than I had ever been, because of how tender he was being. Because of how he'd pulled his body and spirit back together again in the middle of the night. And because secretly I was pleased that after all of this was done—the reunion and the rocking and the tears and the pillows thrown to the floor—he would be gone again. Then I could use as much or as little of the bed as I wanted to, once all the sheets were tucked back in and pulled tight against the darkness of the night, the window shades in our bedroom drawn just so. Like usual.

Kirk and I touch each other in a different way when I come to him in his new place. The light there is dim but steady. We can see shadows on each other, and this makes us slower. The first time I came to him, that night when I found the place while drunk and disbelieving, he had smiled at me in a warm, welcoming way.

No "I told you so." But also no sense of desperation, the way he is when he comes to me in our bed.

He has stopped drinking. I didn't believe him at first. I searched his place once while he was asleep. Not a single drop. His meanness is different now that he's dry. It's honest and cautious, almost curious. "You're different in this light," he said to me the other night from his seat at the chipped linoleum table in the corner, watching me hover near his little mattress. "What's different?" I asked, feeling naked even though I hadn't taken off my wet clothes yet. I was shivering. "You haven't aged at all," he said, watching me. "But there's something different. I can see it in this light." I looked down at the skin on the tops of my hands. "Your face," he said sharply. "That makeup adds too much." I reached up for my eyes. Before dipping below the surface of the river, my eyelashes had been bristly and hard and heavy with mascara. They felt soft now. I knew that my face was a mess. "You're making yourself older," Kirk said. He walked across the tiny expanse of the single room he now lives in and pulled himself against me on the mattress. "Don't do that," he said, pulling my hand away from my face in a gentle way. "Why do you do that?"

I shook my head because I didn't have a single thing to say back to him. Jean and I had actually gone out that night instead of hanging out in my tiny living room. I was a little drunk, which I usually am when I visit Kirk at his place. But I had felt bold after spending time with Jean at one of the dumpy bars just a few blocks away from the river. And that's rare, feeling any kind of boldness when I come to see Kirk. So rare, it slipped away as soon as he touched me.

On those catfish fry nights at our place, my husband never had as many stories as Walt did. Kirk would save them for when we were alone in bed, about to drift off. He once told me about a drowned crow. He told me about a long, red carp folded up like an accordion inside the belly of a catfish. His stories were often only a sentence long. Sometimes just one breath: an empty turtle shell buried in the silt.

My mother died when I was five, and I swear to you that my father and I never discussed it. Because of that, she wasn't a quiet ghost. Because of that, regular, everyday things seemed holy sometimes. Like the drying ring of water left behind on a tabletop by a glass of iced tea. Or the smell of an old, favorite pillow when you press into it and that's all you breathe. I know that my father was taken by those kinds of moments, too. Maybe that's why he refused to get involved in noodling. He couldn't face any kind of legacy that dealt with the dark, swallowed up pit of the unknown like that. Not when he was trying to stay away from those sudden moments of ambush that grief and fear threw into his everyday life like the sharpest and swiftest of poisoned arrows.

Jean still spends one or two evenings at my place most weeks. She never has much to say for the first hour or so. She nods her head ferociously as soon as I open my mouth. I'm afraid her head will snap clean off her delicate neck like a dandelion bud. When she's had enough to drink, that's when I finally hear her talk.

"That man who took Kirk's place at the new elementary school building site over in Sheridan is huge," Jean says one night, buzzed from a few glasses of wine. "I couldn't imagine taking that on in bed."

"Hmm," I say. If I stay quiet and still, I've learned, then she'll keep talking.

"But actually I can imagine it. Kirk was so skinny, and this man is so big. I've seen him. He could take the breath out of you."

We sit in my living room and pass wine bottles back and forth, pouring just a little bit into our glasses each time. Hours pass this way, back and forth, and Jean talks about Kirk like he's her own lost husband, as if Walt isn't around breathing and loving her. She'll hint at infidelity, like mentioning the fat guy who got Kirk's job. I know she'll never cheat on Walt to get back at him. Maybe she's sad about that.

The first night Kirk came back to me, he made me swear not to tell anyone. Sometimes I feel like telling Jean so she'll stop talking about my husband like he's dead and gone, like she owns a piece of him somehow because of all that drunk talking she does. She'll cross her bony ankles and smile in her sad way, wondering why I can't mourn and remember my husband the way she does.

Jean comes over and we drink, and then I let her drive home. I watch her inch cautiously down my driveway and then shoot off into the empty street, weightless.

I have no idea what Kirk does when he's alone in his place. There isn't a television. No books. While he's sleeping, I look for a radio tucked away in the one cupboard above the little sink. I look for one in the empty closet. Even behind the toilet that sits, exposed, in a corner of the room. My husband isn't a man who can sit still without distractions. He needs a beer in his hand, the front door propped open so he can hear the desperate whinny of our only neighbors yelling from all the way down the street, the eleven o'clock news turned up high. Each time I find him down here, he's sitting on the bed or at the table with empty hands. I want to give him a nice piece of wood and a pocket knife. He's got nothing to whittle away at but time.

After Kirk falls asleep, I sit on the edge of his twin mattress and stare across the room at the windowless, fake-wood paneling. I shiver when I imagine him doing the exact same thing. Sometimes I cry. But mostly this is a calm, peaceful place for me. I'll admit that I'm jealous. My husband got here first.

Walt stopped by the house one night a week or so after Kirk's funeral. He didn't say where Jean was. We sat on my back porch and shared a warm beer. I had never spent any time alone with him before. I watched his profile as he stared into the edges of dusk. I could feel something buzzing off of him, a warmth spreading from his sandy, tousled hair. I watched his huge hand bring the can of beer to his lips. I couldn't think of what to say. I didn't know, yet, that Kirk was still around. For all I know, he could have been hiding in the thick patch of sugar maples, watching us. I often wonder now if that night would have been different if I had known that Kirk wasn't gone. I like to think that I would have pulled Walt up against me. I would have asked him to comfort me that way. He can be so quiet. I would have taken the warm beer from his hands and pulled him onto the worn porch planks, for anyone to see.

"I was jealous of all the cat grabbing the two of them would go out and do," Jean says, sitting on my living room floor with her back pressed into my knees. It's almost dawn, and I'm not sure if she'll drive home this time, or if she'll curl up on my couch. I'll let her drive if she decides to leave.

"Weren't you jealous?" she asks.

I don't say anything. I sit back in the couch and let her rest there against my knees and shins. Walt hasn't been noodling since Kirk disappeared. He says he doesn't think he could ever do it again. I don't think it's just because he's sad about Kirk. I think he's scared, too.

"When I first met Walt, he tried to point out his noodling scars. He thought it would impress me." Jean rolls her head back and sighs. "I was impressed," she tells the ceiling.

I think about Kirk's scars. The oldest ones have healed into faint, white tracks on his forearms. When he first pointed them out to me, just after we met, I had to squint to see them. Kirk got angry, thinking I was trying to poke fun. He didn't understand how the whole idea of what those men did lit me up inside. After we started sleeping together I'd trace the halo of rough, callused skin that circles his left wrist while he slept, a beautiful, pale bracelet.

My head feels like it's twirling against the back of the couch. It's the wine, and it's Jean sitting here on my living room floor resting against me.

"He's cheated on me more than once," Jean says. "Did you know that?"

"No," I lie.

I know she's crying. I don't hear it, but I can tell. Lately, Jean's been talking about Walter and the hard times they have been through. There's been a subtle shift in what she's mourning, from my dead husband to her live one. Her sadness, along with the wine, is like a warm blanket. I could close my eyes.

But then Jean lifts her head and pulls away so that she can face me. There's a confrontation in her eyes that kills everything.

"You miss him," she says.

Strands of Jean's thin hair are caught in her lips. She doesn't care. She could spring up on me, her palms pressed into the floor like that. She is desperate to pull things back around to Kirk, to me and my dead husband.

"Yeah," I say.

Jean's face falls. Her eyes get wet again. She's glad that she can get me to admit this one little thing. She gives me one of her sad smiles. Here we are, each of us husband-less in our own way.

I could tell her. I could make her believe me. I could drive her to the abandoned river bank and pull her into the cool, quiet water. I could make her feel inside that dark hole set into the far bank. Then she would experience the most curious sensation of all. Just when you think your lungs should fill with water, you breathe in a way that doesn't feel like breathing at all. It feels good. I would show her my husband when she finally opened her eyes. I would show her his place, and she would realize that we aren't the same anymore in what's missing from our lives. Because here my husband is, sitting in a dark room with a naked toilet in the corner, beneath that little, snaky river. Beneath all of us coming home every night after working our hard jobs. Our town, and

Ohio, and all the rest of it, pressing on top of him. My husband is faithful. He is down there with the cats—those big fish roaming like lazy lions, empty of fear.

Kirk sits up in our bed. When he visits me at home, he insists on leaving before morning comes. His shirt is right there, bundled next to his pillow. I watch him pull his head through, then his arms.

"None of the guys have been coming out to the river," he says.

I nod and wonder how he knows this.

"Not since you disappeared."

"They're missing the best part of the season," Kirk says, pulling on his shoes.

It is the best part. The water is cooling off. The catfish that are still guarding their nests are even more desperate than usual to protect them, to fan the eggs and get them hatched before it's too cold. They put up the best fight just before fall sets in. The weather is getting to me, too. When I go to Kirk's place now, I sometimes begin to choke on the cold water. The river will freeze over by January. And somehow I know that my husband won't bother trying to break through until well after the first thaw of spring.

"I want to tell Walt," Kirk says.

My breath is quick. All I can do is stare.

"Do you hear me?" he asks, standing at the foot of the bed. "I want to tell him."

There is a threat in my husband's voice, but I ignore it.

"Why?" I ask.

"He should know."

My husband kneels on the bed in front of me like a child. His face is in shadows beneath all of that dark hair.

"I could show him my place," he says.

"But you can't just show yourself to him," I say. "You're dead to him, a ghost. He's been mourning you."

"Nessa."

Kirk's voice washes over my bare shoulders. I pull the blanket up around me. He won't let me argue with him. He pushes me back and lies on top of me. I feel his breathing change. He is tense, trying to convince himself of something. He isn't on top of me; he's on top of a raft, leaning over the edge and trying to see all that is rushing beneath him. I can feel him swallow. He doesn't feel safe here, with the day about to reach in through the windows.

My husband's depression is a darkness he can't tell me about when he opens his mouth in the middle of the night and then doesn't say a word. There's a sadness that is older than him. That's what I think about when Kirk holds on too tight.

I let him fall asleep. Dawn snakes through the cracks in the window shades and curls there on his back. When he wakes, he stares at me before pulling himself up. He looks around the room for reminders and reassurances that this is worth it, waking next to me after the night has disappeared.

After my father died, I looked up catfish lore. I looked for stories about big fish pulling children off the shore, swallowing them whole. Instead I found happy stories of little children being rescued by giant, whale-sized cats. In ancient times, the Japanese thought that the Earth, a rock, rested on the back of a catfish. There were gentle earthquakes when he shook his bellowing fins. Where I'm from, in the heart of this country, there is an ancient myth about a tribe of catfish that decided to spear down a herd of moose one night while they were eating sweet grasses that grew along the shore. The tribe failed and they were trampled by the angry moose. Now these freshwater predators have wide, flat heads to remind them of the failure of their past hunt. And that is why the cats fight so fiercely when these men reach into their dark nests. That is why when a cat is latched onto your arm, you feel like you could be at the very center of terror and dread. That's what I've been told. You can feel it beneath the surface of the murky water, their vow to never let go.

Something broke inside of Jean last night. She was talking about Walter again, about how good he is to her and how she needs to finally forgive him.

Jean said: "The past is the past."

Her tears started then, with that sad, soap opera statement. And then she couldn't say anything more because she was crying so much. Her entire face was wet, tears dripping onto her neck and rolling beneath her T-shirt. Her sobbing was soft and hollow, like the sound of someone gently blowing over the top of an old-fashioned Coke bottle. All I could think while she was sitting there on my couch, her shirt starting to soak through, was: If only Walter could hear me make that same sound.

Eventually Jean was able to tell me, half through words and half through gestures, that she wanted me to help her into the shower. She did calm down a bit once the bathroom had filled with steam. She looked hopeful, as if a shower could wash away the tears that hadn't come yet.

Jean was full of wine and grief, and I had to hold her by her waist while she stood in the spray of the shower, one of my legs in the tub. The wet seam of my jeans cut into my thigh. When Jean was finally quiet, she looked dead standing there. Peaceful. I held onto her and stared at what Walt comes home to every night: the glistening kneecaps and the heaving, sad chest. When I see Jean and Walt together now I watch the way they move so easily. Walt's big hands at her hips when he kisses her on the forehead. With Jean standing there in my bathtub, I thought of the long, awkward stretch of Kirk next to me in bed, how even the way he breathes while he's asleep makes me nervous.

After the shower, Jean wanted to drive home. I let her. She was still wet, her hair clinging to her skull like mine does when I get home from Kirk's place. I helped her pull her tear-soaked shirt back down over her head. She was cold when she climbed into her car. I know it's inappropriate for Jean to out-grieve me, a woman with a dead husband. But I don't care.

⌣

THE particular river that I've been describing, it pulls from all directions. I wonder if Kirk and Walter ever noticed this while they were out there wading along miles and miles of muddy bank, trying to read the shore. Once you step into the water, your body wants to go everywhere. And that is exactly how I feel tonight before I even pick up the phone. My fingertips trace over every number. My heart pushes against the inside of me. I am tired. An aching, aching tired.

When Walt picks up I ask him to come to my place. I don't ask him to lie to Jean, to make up some story, but I know he will. My thighs throb when I see Walt's headlights cut through the windows. I'm always lightheaded after dipping below the water and then opening my eyes to the dim, sheltered light of my husband's place. I feel this way now, with Walt in the doorway. He says, "Nessa."

I do this so easily. I lay him down near the potted, dusty ferns beside the rocking chair. I expect to be able to read Jean all over Walt's face and hands, but she's not there. I'm sure there are moments, pockets within this world, when Walt can be just as mean as my husband.

"I miss him," Walt says, his chest pressed into my back, his breathing still heavy.

Of course there is a sadness when I try to think about my mother and all the things that my father and I never said to each other about her. But I think that sadness is more than just the emptiness of her being gone. I think there was a sadness surrounding her even when she was alive, during those first few years of my life. That's it, I think. That's the one secret my father never wanted me to know.

My father's stories no longer frighten me. When Kirk first disappeared and I thought he was dead, I went to work at the daycare and watched over the children in a daze. They grabbed at my hands because I was so quiet and slow. Even now when I'm at work, surrounded by those children with smudged, open faces, something inside my heart shifts sometimes. I allow myself to imagine lining them up neatly along the river's shore, watching them get swallowed up one by one. Forcing my father's stories to come true.

monster drinks chocolate milk

THE MONSTER WHO has been haunting me since I was a kid is depressed. We sit on my kitchen counter in the middle of the night and drink chocolate milk. This is so awkward, he says. Don't worry about it, I say. But really, he says, I feel kind of bad about this. I shake my head, hoping he can see that there's nothing to feel bad about. I mean, the whole scaring me shitless in the middle of the night a few times a month since I was a toddler. Yeah, go ahead and feel bad about that, I think to myself. But not this whole depression thing. I know it's hard to think through this clearly, I want to tell him, but this isn't your fault. The two of us stay quiet for a long time, sipping our chocolate milk and watching our legs dangle below us. I guess I should tell you what my monster looks like. I've never really had a chance to look at him and study him before. But now sitting next to him here on my kitchen counter under the hard fluorescent light I see that he isn't that big. In fact, if he were a man, he'd be considered pretty short. He would probably have a complex about it. His skin is rough and cracked, which I guess I would have expected for a monster. His eyes are tiny and rheumy and gross. He's got dark bags under his little eyes, and I wonder if this has something to do with his depression. Or if it's just a monster thing. I've got this anxiety, he says. His glass is empty, and so I hop down to make him more chocolate milk. I don't even ask him if he wants more. I'm anxious all the time, he says. I stir and stir as fast as I can, trying to break up the glob of Hershey's syrup that's stuck to the bottom of the glass. Anxiety is like a beast, he says, and I nod so he can see that I get the metaphor.

My monster says he's hungry. I open the fridge and try to think of something I could whip together and somehow impress a guest with. He sidles up next to me (or lurches, actually—monsters really do lurch) and starts helping himself. He pulls out an old, expired bag of shredded cheese I've been ignoring for months. He starts stacking various sized Tupperware containers in his arms, and I have no idea what's in those things. He sets everything on the counter between us and then he eats all of it. He doesn't even look at the stuff. He just eats it. I'm so embarrassed. Some of the stuff I don't even recognize anymore. Some of the stuff I have to fight not to gag when I see it or smell it. I'm embarrassed, but then I realize that monsters probably love this kind of stuff, that he's probably relieved that I'm such a lazy slob. When he's finally full and happy (well, he's *depressed,* but you know what I mean) I feel some of the awkwardness that was between us before melt away a little bit. I feel like I could say anything to him right now, and so I tell him that I'm embarrassed. Not about the old, gross food in my refrigerator, though. What I say is, I'm too embarrassed to tell people that you still come to me at night. I say, I'm too embarrassed to tell people how afraid of you I still am. My monster nods his head softly. He doesn't need to say anything, and he knows it. I wish that I could keep this moment forever. I wish it were a tangible thing. Could you do it? I ask him. Could you scare me? Here? he asks. I nod. And so he gives me the look. He just turns his head and does it. Everything happens like usual, in the exact same sequence. It doesn't matter that it is not dark and that I am not curled into myself on top of my bed. He looks at me, and the horrible fear falls over my head and breaks open like an egg with a shell that has already been cracked—just a tiny, hairline fracture—and ready. There is the paralysis, of course. There is the exploding heart and the collapsed lungs and the dryness sucking at my eyes like a horrible, evil Hoover. I feel it all. I feel the things that I could never tell you and I almost fall right off the counter. But then he stops. He looks back down at his dangling, short legs. He is so sad. I can see that now. He is more sad than he is monster. And now I wonder if he'll ever do it again, look at me like that. And I feel crazy, because I wonder if I would miss it. Nice curtains, he says, staring at the cheap fabric hanging above the sink, which will look so chintzy in the light of day.

Before he leaves, my monster insists on doing the dishes. I try to talk him out of it. I lie and say that I enjoy doing dishes, that it relaxes me. I point out the dishwasher, but he just shrugs and fills up the left side of the sink with hot water and suds. He washes everything by hand and is surprisingly thorough. He takes his time. He won't even let me dry. He's got a few, angry tufts of hair scattered across his skull, and I stare at them while he does the dishes. I think about how if those tufts of hair were thick and luscious, and if he were a woman, a human woman right here in this room with me at this very minute, drinking chocolate milk and bravely scavenging through my old, inappropriate leftovers in the middle of the night, I would be glad. And she would be beautiful.

vanishing point

IT'S AGAINST THE rules. Glenn slips into my sleeping bag in the middle of the night. We have to be quiet, which I don't mind. We've been told that the sleeping bags are meant to help us feel like we are back inside our mothers' wombs again. But I think we are given sleeping bags because this place used to be a camping outfitters and why waste supplies that are already on hand, no matter how old and musty they are. The first time Glenn came to me in the dark, I unzipped my bag as slowly and as quietly as possible and he just stood there and watched without a single trace of anticipation on his shadowed face. In the mornings, he passes me the dented kettle of coffee or the tin plate loaded with thick-cut bacon without saying a word, and no one else pressed together at the old pine table seems to notice a thing. The whole point of being here is to detach ourselves from what we have lost and what we need to grieve. And here Glenn and I are, attaching ourselves to each other every night, over and over again. Totally against the rules. He is lean and slow and so good at being quiet. When we are pressed together in the stale heat of my sleeping bag

I run through some of the mantra we've been taught to hammer into ourselves:

I love myself.

I accept myself.

I'm important.

I deserve good things.

I forgive myself.

Over and over again, every night, Glenn comes to me and I forgive myself.

Before coming out here, I knew to expect the lakes scattered everywhere and the mosquitoes and the huge pieces of rock jutting out of the earth. I had stared at Arthur's little pamphlet for hours and had gone on-line to search "wilderness" and "Minnesota Boundary Waters." But what I didn't expect was the disorientating floating feeling I'd have being surrounded by so many bodies of dark, connected water. I didn't expect the mosquitoes to attack in swarms, the whinny of their multitudinous approach like the screaming of banshees. I didn't expect the orange and green lichen to cling to the jutting rocks like bright beards. I didn't expect the loon's call to sound lonely and lovely all at once. I didn't know I'd love or even notice the people who live in this pocket of the world, the ones who have lived here for a lifetime. If I lived here, I think I'd drive to the nearest town every day, which is an hour from camp, and fill myself with the thick malts and fried cheese curds that they serve in the tiny restaurants there. Then I would sit back and wait to feel it—a slow takeover of the introverted good cheer that people like Arthur possess. The mysterious thing that must keep them insulated and safe during the blind, cold winters that they have out here. I'm envious of all of it. And I'm surprised by this, how my mouth waters.

Here at camp, it's the ones without any kind of substantial proof of a lost twin who seem so certain and who buy into all of Arthur's theories without hesitation. Cathy says she's had a strange numbness in her limbs each morning since as far back as she can remember, and that's all the proof she needs. For Frank, it's his eczema. Sheila has bad breath and Nancy has an extra pinky toe. Dan has a mole exactly on the center of his left knee cap. They look at these random, insignificant things and whole-heartedly grant them all the significance in the world. Look at this here. See this? This is the reason for my loneliness. My depression. My anxiety and anger and fear. This is the reason for the empty hole sloshing around inside of my soul.

When I was eighteen months old, I started falling whenever I walked. I'd land on my bottom and cry and cry, my face red with pain in spite of the padding of my diaper and the thick shag carpeting in my parents' home. My mother noticed a redness above my spine, just the faintest hint of something tough and swollen beneath my skin. Of course she was full of a sudden, vicious worry that only mothers can possess, the kind of worry that is sharper and more exact than intuition. She demanded tests, and there were tests. There was a biopsy and surgery. But it wasn't cancer, the darkest thing huddled there in the hot pocket of my mother's worry. It was something she never could have imagined: a benign cyst made up of a jumbled mess of hair and teeth and skin. The surgeons who removed the tumor told my mother that she had been pregnant with twins. That things had gotten a bit "complicated" very early in the pregnancy and I had absorbed the other fetus into my own body before it could finish develop-ing into anything near human. It fused to the bottom of my spine, a mess of cells. Not really a twin, they told her. Just the makings of one. On the second day of camp, Arthur asked us to choose a body part and imagine that's where the absorption of our twin occurred when we were fetuses. I chose my right elbow instead of my lower back. I don't know why. Maybe because my elbow is easier to see. All of us campers catch each other glancing at these random parts of ourselves, trying to visualize and believe.

I don't know what body part Glenn chose as his lost twin's point of absorption. Maybe one of his bony wrists or the soft, delicate point where his hair trails into a V on the back of his neck. When I touch him, I feel like I'm intruding. I want to know which part of himself he has chosen to be secret and sacred. I would never touch it.

Arthur has told us that there is something swimming beneath the threshold of our memory, a primordial kind of awareness where our earliest experiences have been logged and stored permanently. Of course none of us remember floating around inside of the warm viscous-ness of our mother's womb, but the experience is there nonetheless, tucked deep into the folds of our psyche. Arthur says that some of us might claim to remember, but we are lying to ourselves. It's about something altogether different from remembering. And that's what we are supposed to get at while we are here at Vanishing Point, way out in the middle of the Minnesota Boundary Waters Wilderness. One of the rivers that my shuttle from the Minneapolis Airport crossed during the day-long drive to camp was called Baptism River. Sometimes Arthur seems like a preacher, no matter how quiet he gets. No matter the fact that he has taken our money for two weeks of crazy jibber jabber about the Primal Wound of the Womb and Emotional Freedom Technique and Conception Guilt and Womb Twin Survivor. He does seem tapped into something that I don't think any of us could ever recognize, no matter how long we stayed or how much money we shelled over.

The first project Arthur had us do when we arrived—before we were assigned an old sleeping bag or given time to unpack our things—was cut a photo of a person out of a magazine. He had a random collection piled up on the table where we take our meals, and many of the issues of *Vogue* and *Good Housekeeping* and *People* and *Self* had already been picked over by previous campers. Arthur asked us to cut out a face that embodied some quality of our lost twin. The other campers took their time, agonizing over issues of *Time* and *Maxim* as they tried to narrow down their choices. I chose the first person I saw when I opened up a worn issue of *Ladies' Home Journal,* a plus-sized model smiling bravely in a simple black bra and panty set. We wear the pictures around our necks, slipped into waterproof plastic sleeves. Glenn was the only other camper who made his choice quickly, and when I saw the picture in his badge—a teenaged goth-looking model who is all skin and bones—I thought maybe he was joking. I thought there might be the relief of whispering with him at the campfire about how outrageous this all is, who could ever believe it. But he's serious about all of this, I've realized. Just like everyone else here, he's got his reasons to believe. He's left handed. He had a stutter as a kid. He's miserable without the companionship of recreational drug use.

I've started slipping into my sleeping bag naked each night. I tell myself that I'm trying to give Arthur's theories a fair shot, that maybe I'll better be able to imagine my return to the primordial womb if I don't have a stitch on me. Really it just makes things easier when Glenn comes. Trying to wriggle out of my clothing with both of us pressed in there is a bit awkward and jerky, nothing at all like the sex itself. There are only two sleeping cabins. When Glenn comes over from his, he's not too careful about keeping the door from creaking and whining. He shuffles over to my cot and it sounds like someone trying to sweep away dead leaves. But no one else ever seems to be awake but me. Maybe everyone else's sleeping bag has some kind of spell on it that places them into an unconscious state much deeper than sleep, a place where Arthur's therapeutic work can continue in the farthest reaches of the brain. Maybe my sleeping bag is defunct. And Glenn's. The two of us are quiet, but I don't know that we need to be. Frank snores aggressively across from us. Cathy is stiff as a corpse in the bunk above me. And here I am with a stranger pressed into my sleeping bag, feeling just as sleepy and lost as everyone else in this tiny cabin. When Glenn arrives in the middle of the night, a cloud of mosquitoes comes in with him. We disappear completely inside of my sleeping bag, pulling the top all the way over our heads. Still, we can hear the solid, patient whine of anticipation just above us.

Arthur is small and wizened and decades and decades old. He runs the place like the tightest of ships. There is no questioning the schedule that is posted next to the front door of each sleeping cabin. We move together in a herd from skin diving sessions in the little lake to breakfast to group therapy to quiet journaling time to lunch to arts and crafts to individual sessions with Arthur and on and on and on. Although the property is well over three hundred years old (it used to be a French fur trading camp), everything has been kept in working order. Arthur runs a single crank generator for the radio and the refrigerator and the few bare light bulbs scattered about the shack-like buildings. He is religious about it and says the place has never run out of power. You would expect him to have huge, bulging muscles from all the time he spends turning the little wheel of that generator, but he's so small. None of us understand it. And we don't understand why a man like Arthur would choose to run a camp like Vanishing Point. During therapy sessions and workshops he pulls stories out of us like easy, silk threads, but he has never said a word about himself in any deep, personal regard. Maybe this is because that kind of information would distract us from our own work here. But the mystery surrounding Arthur is what's most distracting of all. We sit around the dying campfire after Arthur has left, no longer swatting at the mosquitoes because of the warm buzz of the whiskey that Sheila smuggled in. Glenn glares at us with a hard smile of abstinence on his face, and we try to piece together what Arthur's story might be. Maybe he was married once, and he lost his wife when they were young. Maybe he was a secret operative for the CIA and he retired out here in the wilderness to try to escape the horrible things he had done and seen. Most of the campers are certain that Arthur himself must have lost a twin before he was born. But I don't buy into that. I think that this entire program that Arthur has put together out here is a random obsession for him and it's as easy as that. Maybe he came across an old issue of *National Geographic* at the dentist's office and opened it up to a story about us, survivors of a vanished womb twin. Maybe he was taking a series of old fashioned correspondence courses through the mail and the one on Vanishing Twin Syndrome caught his eye, the sketches on the front of the pamphlet of the kidney-bean-sized fetuses floating in a ghost womb. Yes, Arthur could have made up all of the theories and techniques that he teaches us here. But I think all of this is something that he himself bought into. Something that he studied up on and then chose to believe in. And if he was ever lonely in his life, how can he be now? We send in our deposits and take flights from all over the country to get here and sit with him in old aluminum chairs on the dock, trying to shoo the ungodly bugs away as nonchalantly as possible because Arthur here just sits and takes it without the slightest flinch.

On the first day of camp we were all issued T-shirts with the Vanishing Point logo, a rough sketch of an empty road viewed head on, so that the two parallel yellow lines in the center of the road seem to come together and merge into one single line that shoots off into the horizon. Arthur says that's the vanishing point, where two separate things have the illusion of coming together. But why name the camp Vanishing Point when he asks us to discover the opposite of that union, to learn how to push our invisible twins out in a gentle kind of exorcism? What would you call that? I couldn't begin to design a T-shirt logo for that.

During group therapy sessions, I often find myself staring out the old, billowed screen windows at the rocks and trees and water that make up this landscape. Sometimes I panic at the thought of being in a place where I could get lost so easily. What if I tried to turn this whole experience into a fairytale? I could fill a little pack with a few smart provisions and then set out into the thick fingers of pine and birch. I'd drop little crumbs from the hard, waxy biscuits that Arthur sets out each morning and none of us touch. The moose and the black bears and the wolves and the foxes and the otters would eat those crumbs and no one, not even Arthur, would be able to track me. The open darkness that must rest at the center of all of this forest would swallow me whole.

During art therapy, Bill tells us how he has two separate wardrobes. One for his fat, masculine self and one for his thin, feminine self. Genie describes the telepathy she shares with her dead twin. Frank tells us about his issues with money. We are supposed to be drawing two pictures of our mother's womb. The first one of before the loss of our twin and the second one of after. The crayons are broken and old and smell like a school library. Sheila shades her mother's womb (the after) a deep, furious purple and says that she suspects that she is electrically sensitive. She says her watches always stop working soon after she buys them and that streetlights often go out when she walks beneath them. Tom tells us that he lost a sister in the womb. He is quiet and gentle, with long, beautiful hair that all of the female campers envy. Tom says he wants to give birth to his lost sister. And during this loaded, intensely personal moment I stare out the screen windows and watch the ripples on the black lake. I've seen campers paddling past in their canoes. Most of the people who camp out here in this wilderness know what to expect. They come with only one or two tight packs and a lot of good sense. But I've seen some clueless people paddle by, fumbling with the folds of big, fluttering maps, their canoes weighted down with huge coolers and too much expensive, useless gear. Arthur tells us stories of people who have gotten lost after going too far out for their level of experience. They lose track of the portages—the little, rugged paths that connect the endless web of lakes. The smart ones don't panic. They stay put and patiently wait days, or even weeks, for another camper to appear. Or they set fire to the scraggly trees on one of the little rock islands that dot this country and wait for a fishing guide or a Department of Natural Resources officer to fly overhead and see the thin, desperate trail of smoke. But what about the ones who aren't smart? The ones who panic?

We were issued a mask for skin diving when we arrived. The dives in the lake take place early each morning, well before breakfast. When I hold my breath and peer beneath the surface of the lake for that first shocking glimpse of the day, I'm so hungry and cold that my vision is sharp and precise. I'm able to focus in on each tiny bit of silt that's been stirred up from the lake's mucky bottom. Arthur has been training us to hold our breath for longer and longer chunks of time each morning. The goal is to be able to hold our breath long enough to dive down to an old wrecked car at the bottom of the lake. Arthur has no idea how long the car has been down there or how it got there, but he uses it for the Final Ritual of Letting Go at the end of camp. He says that the breathing techniques we've been learning during our morning dives will allow us to push our twins out of us during that final, difficult dive down to the bottom of the lake. In the mornings I slip off of the dock into the cold water and gasp and sputter while placing the big mask over my eyes and nose. We tread water and stare at each other before beginning the breathing exercises, looking like a swarm of silly insects. Everything down there is brown and yellow and green and strange. There isn't much to see. The endless hulk of rocks piled solidly together. The quick golden-silver flash of a bony northern pike turning away. A dead frog floating with its limbs spread wide in surprise. Magda can't swim and she has been at Vanishing Point for years, watching group after group of campers go through the two week program and then finish their final dive. There are rumors that she came as a camper and then stayed on as Arthur's lover and that this is why she has become a permanent fixture. But she seems nothing like a secret lover. She goes through all the group sessions and workshops right alongside us. She's just as clueless about Arthur as we are. She watches us each morning from one of the aluminum chairs on top of the warped dock, bobbing there above us with endless longing and envy.

Glenn and I are out picking blueberries and dodging black flies before this afternoon's workshop on The Healing Fetus. We kneel next to the little shrubs behind the canoe racks and collect the tiny berries in plastic baggies, hoping our pitiful offering will somehow spruce up Arthur's horrible cooking. He insists on making all of the meals and won't allow any of us to volunteer in the cramped kitchen. He enjoys feeding us, his strange flock.

"These are so tiny," Glenn says. "It would take years to pick enough for one single pie."

Glenn and I have exchanged very few words over the past couple weeks. Nothing is said when he crawls into my sleeping bag at night. He wants to be nonchalant out here in the open. He wants some small talk beneath the hard sun. But he's jumpy and wired. When he grabs for a berry, the tail-end of a snaky looking tattoo pokes out of his shirtsleeve. I wish I could wrap him up in a sleeping bag right now. Glenn says little during group therapy sessions. When he does talk, he refers to his drug use as if it's such an ordinary task—doing the dishes, sorting the mail, shooting up. I don't know the exact kind of detox he is facing. He should go somewhere legit that is designed to handle that kind of thing. The setting out here is too severe and wild and haunting with its crisp air and water, the land rolling and spiking away from us in every direction like something completely unmappable and unnameable.

I wish I could tell Glenn something about myself, even something tiny and trivial. I've been holding back from everyone here, including Arthur. During therapy, I've lied and made up an alcoholic, verbally abusive father. I've given myself two evil step mothers and a horrible bout of meningitis in middle school. I've survived earthquakes and car jackings and botched liposuction. All of it lies. I want to tell Glenn something real, because he is so shaky and uncertain. Because he deserves it. Instead I lie.

"I'm here because of my dreams," I say. "They have always felt like someone else's. They have never felt like my own."

Instead of looking at me like I'm crazy, Glenn stares at his little baggy of blueberries and nods.

Besides Magda, who was born alongside the mummified, shriveled body of her undeveloped twin, I'm the only one here who has any kind of legitimate proof of a lost twin. But I've told no one about the cyst that was removed when I was a toddler, not even Arthur. That experience doesn't feel real enough. I think telling that story would be more false than the lies I've been telling since the day I arrived here. Somehow, it would seem more false than the way the other campers lie to themselves during therapy, willing a lost soul mate into their empty lives. And then there would be the jealousy. If the other campers knew about my tumor, they would eye me with something like hate. I'm sure of it.

It isn't true that I haven't thought about my lost twin. Sure, I'm obsessed in my own way. What's it like when I do think about it? It's like when you are going about something ordinary and trivial and then you hear a siren off in the distance—too far off to know if it's a firetruck or an ambulance or a cop car. And you catch yourself closing your eyes and saying something like a prayer. For a split second, before the sting of self-consciousness takes over, you feel connected to everyone in this world.

My cyst could have been on my face. Or up in my nasal cav-
ity. Or tucked inside my brain like a grotesque egg. My cyst could
have lodged itself in my ovaries and waited there for years and
years, dormant until it finally ruptured and insisted that I give
birth, in some kind of bloody fashion, to my own unformed sib-
ling. All of that hair and skin and bits of bone and teeth without
an ounce of soul, why would I want to feel any connection to
that? Sometimes I wonder if I have been living my twin's life all
along. We've all heard those stories about twins separated at birth
who are reunited as adults and realize they have the same husbands and the same dogs and the same sweaters. What if my life,
all of the good and all of the bad, isn't my own? Sometimes I feel
territorial of all of it, even the mistakes and the mundane and
the things that are too impossible to ever say.

It's the morning of the Final Ceremony of Letting Go, and
Arthur asks us to name our womb twins. He doesn't make us
share our names or talk about it with each other. He simply sug-
gests that we think of a name and hold it in our minds and our
hearts. I stare at the face of the plus-sized underwear model that's
sealed in the waterproof pouch around my neck and try to think
of a name. I try to give her Connie or Bess or Sandy. Amy or
Rachel. But she won't take any of those names. She just smiles
back at me, dumb and defiant. A lot of the other campers start
to cry. I can see the exact moment when they think of the right
name. Something shifts in their faces. Arthur is somber. He stands
at the end of the dock and tells us that the womb is an unsafe
and unstable environment. He tells us that we weren't alone and
that our twin was there to support us. "Wombs can carry grief
and fear older than time," Arthur tells us. "You were not alone."

The final dive isn't hard. Arthur's intense training has taught
us well. He takes small groups of us out to the spot above the
sunken car in an aluminum boat with a sputtering outboard mo-

tor. After he drops the anchor we take turns going down. I suck in one succinct pull of air and then go. The rusty hulk of the car is hard to make out in the endless brown water, but it doesn't take long to spot the orange piece of plastic flag that Arthur tied to the antenna who knows how long ago. I do as I've been told and let go of my plastic badge just above the driver's seat so that my twin can drive away to somewhere else, away from me and into her own life. The badge just floats there and then starts to drift away from the wreck. But I like to imagine that all of the badges end up sinking into the driver's seat. I like to believe that they are piled up there, all of those ghost faces wilted and silted over with time. I don't get a chance to linger and wait for some kind of change to occur down there in the abyss of the lake. My lungs ache and sting and I can't help rushing back up to the sur-real looking surface.

Tonight Glenn and I get high. When he comes to me, he pulls me out of my sleeping bag and he waits for me to get dressed. We walk out to the dock. He places two or three tiny pills in the palm of my hand. I can barely see them because it's so dark. They feel like nothing when I swallow. Glenn is already somewhere else, rigid and loose at the same time. I hold onto his arm while I wait to feel whatever it is that he is feeling. The quiet, economical sex we've been having has not been enough to distract Glenn from this. My head starts to contract and expand and I can't stand it. It's not the high—a sweetly sick, sharp soaring—that I mind. It's watching Glenn betray himself. Watching him give in to what he came all the way out here to fight against and avoid. And here I am dipping my hand in right next to his. Glenn is one of the mark-less ones with no tangible proof of a lost twin. He's got a miserable life. That's all. Standing next to him on the dock, my head swirls away from us and I wish that I could turn him into my lost twin. I hate how forced I've let so many things in my life feel, and I wonder if that forced feeling is a true symptom of all of this bullshit that I've paid two thousand dollars to swallow out here in the middle of this wild bit of country.

I'm in the water and it takes me a few moments to realize this. I'm not panicking and sputtering and drowning. My legs and arms maintain a confident, efficient stroke. I let myself disappear beneath the surface and I hold my breath for a very long time. When I come up, I see Arthur holding a lantern and peering out at the dock. He sees Glenn standing there, just at the edge, and he sees me treading water and he knows. I'm high on something. Who knows what. And I want little, old Arthur's vision to be altered for a moment, too.

We had to fill out a survey and send it in with our deposit in order to register for camp. We had to rate our loneliness on a scale of one to ten. We had to remember and count the number of stuffed animals that we slept with as children. Broken bones and break ups. Sexual identity. Posture. Suicide attempts. Loss. Rate your loss on a scale of one to ten.

When I get out of the water, I'm still treading and floating. I don't strip naked. I don't change into dry clothes. I find Arthur in the tiny shack that houses the crank generator, not much bigger than the portapotties. "I'm here," I say. My voice comes from somewhere outside of me. I want Arthur to know that I'm okay. I didn't drown. Who knows about Glenn. For all I know he's still standing there at the end of the dock right at the edge of the world. Arthur is cranking the generator and the little wheel spins silently and efficiently. My head slices into everything. There's a mosquito on my calf, piercing me over and over again. It takes me so long to realize what that stinging could be. "Sorry," I say. Because there are no drugs allowed at Vanishing Point. No sex. Just healing and coming to terms and casting aside. Arthur keeps cranking, and I shiver and wonder if I could shake off this high, if it might evaporate. But until it does, I feel brave. And so I ask, "Why do you do all of this?" Arthur keeps cranking, but he looks at me. His face is dried up and kind as always.

I know that he used to run this place as a camping outfitter. He used to send people out into this wilderness with powdered milk and sleeping bags and slabs of bacon and cheese that had been smoked for so long they wouldn't need to be refrigerated for years. He sent people out with top secret tips on the best fishing spots for walleye, and pulleys and long pieces of rope to suspend food packs high in the air between two trees, away from snooping bears. Now he runs Vanishing Point and keeps us here, tucked in safe and tight at base camp, doing all the searching and exploring on the inside. When I ask him about why he does all this, I expect him to go off on one of his old song and dances about the Trauma of the Womb or Detachment Narratives. But he doesn't. He tells me about the ama divers, women who live on islands off the coast of Japan. Since at least the third century, these women have been skin diving for shellfish and edible seaweed. They hold their breath and swim to the bottom of the sea, placing whatever they bring back up with them in wooden tubs that float on the surface of the water. Most of the women dive topless. They are better divers than the men because of the extra layer of fat that women have. Arthur tells me all of this, and I sort and file the story in my head in a panic, because it feels like something important. It's a story I could never make up, no matter how high or lost I ever got myself.

"I want to go dive with them someday," Arthur says.

His eyes are wet. He has told me a secret. This is the old issue of *National Geographic* that he must have smuggled out of a dentist waiting room and tucked away somewhere, coveted and worn.

When Arthur found me out in the lake tonight, did I look like one of those Japanese divers? When I surfaced and he saw me in the flickering light of his lantern, did I look like I could fit into the grainy, out of focus photographs of an old *National Geographic*? I am thin, but maybe the moonlight gave me the illusion of extra padding on my shoulders and arms. Arthur is more than thin. He is tiny. I wish I could imagine him in the cold morning waters off of the coast of Japan, trying to hold his breath and shivering, thrown around by rough waves. Surrounded by full-busted women with thick voices and strong arms. Those other women would crowd him out with their competent strokes. Arthur is still cranking the generator. How much time he must spend out here in this little shack, spinning away so that this place has just enough electricity running through it to keep going. Maybe he never sleeps. There's an old stationary bike set next to the generator. Arthur sees me staring at it and says, "I hook that up to the generator sometimes. When my arms get tired."

I am high and soaring and I can see it: Arthur pedaling furiously all night long, for an eternity. Arthur told us that something like one out of four natural pregnancies begin as twins. He told us that in some cases one of the twins bleeds out early on. Nothing alarming for the mother, just a little harmless spotting. Or else one fetus is absorbed by the other. Right now I think my head is light enough to believe almost anything. Maybe there is a tight pearl of what could have been tucked away inside of all of us. Maybe the craziest intuitions that some of the people here at Vanishing Point have are dead on, and maybe our twins are solid and real. Maybe there is a pocket of forest deep in this wilderness where all those twins that Arthur's campers expel from themselves end up. I can see them—furrier, happier versions of ourselves. Sleeping in tents and getting things to grow in the rocky soil. Harvesting armfuls of wild rice in the shallows of unmapped lakes. Maybe they never wanted to share our lives. They never wanted to haunt us. Arthur and I could form our own expedition, just the two of us, and try to track them down. But they don't want to be found. And I don't want to find them. I don't think that's why I came out here anyway.

"My husband got sick," I say, and I feel like I am back in the lake again, sucked down by the weight of my clothes. "He didn't get better," I say. Arthur keeps cranking. My little story, what I have just told him, floats sharp and concise in the whirring silence. It floats along with the hundreds of lies that I've told since I arrived at camp, and I will it to become one of them. I want to punch this story into a lie. But there is nothing I can do because I am trapped in the numb, buzzing dome of this high. "He got sick," I say. "That is all." Arthur doesn't ask for more. I feel like I could sink with that bit of story alone. I could sink and drown. Future Vanishing Point campers would take deep breaths and dive down and try to pick bits of my bone out of the old wrecked car. They'd give the bones to Arthur and he would place them in a simple box made out of birch or just an old glass jar set on top of the crank generator. He would glance at the pieces of me every now and then while he turns turns turns.

I will tell you this. My husband and I had a simple story. No faded sleeping bags or mosquitoes or packs of sad, quiet adults doing arts and crafts together each afternoon. No patchwork of rock and water and forest in a wilderness as pure and heartbreaking as silence. It was our life, plain and simple. I would give her this story if I could. My twin. That gritty mass of tissue and mishappened cells. She can have it.

the shopkeeper's tale

ONCE THERE WAS a woman who owned a tiny baby boutique in a small neighborhood of a big city. It was the kind of shop that sells stuff that makes your heart hurt when you look at it: the little, pale sleep sacks as soft as cashmere, the bright, hard bulbs of rubber pacifiers, the artfully worn and ragged stuffed bunnies and cows. When you walk into a place like this, you immediately become overwhelmed by all of the rich color and all of the wool that has been hand-spun in Timbuktu. A bit itchy, maybe, but so beautiful. And oh, the price tag! When you walk into a little baby shop like this one, the displays might seem a bit cramped and haphazard at first glance. But everything, really, has been set up with such care, including the old straw baskets shoved into the corner over there, overflowing with itty bitty washcloths in the shapes of cheerful woodland elves.

The thing about this woman who once owned a tiny baby boutique in a small neighborhood of a big city, and we will call her June—the thing about June was she hated kids. Even babies. Her heart didn't melt when she saw their wet, genuine grins. Her heart didn't melt when they slumbered sweetly against their mothers' chests, folded up like fleshy, warm accordions of all that is good. Her heart didn't melt, even, when she heard the most piercing rise and hiccup of their laughing squeals. No, June did not like babies. And in fact, as I mentioned above, she hated them. But how much, really, can we hold this against her? After all, her store was beautiful and sweet, and she kept the place open late on Wednesdays in the summertime. And June was a woman who could gift wrap things in the simplest yet most magnificent ways. She would ask if your purchase was a gift for someone, and even if you said no, she would often wrap it anyway, just because. She would wrap anything, even a teensy tiny clip-on hair bow (which was going to set you back at least eighteen bucks, mind you). June wrapped those little, precious, overpriced things with such love and care. She used ugly brown paper and little bits of broken ribbon, and the end result was beautiful and perfect. But June hated kids, even babies. And there is no particular reason or cause that we can go back to and revisit deep within the gray folds of her brain. Nothing repressed or tucked away and waiting, trembling there, to rise back to the surface. June simply hated them. And the thing about June was she didn't think about this too much or ask herself why. She simply opened the store each morning and let the early light trickle in and nestle amid all the little, sweet things she had for sale.

And so I wonder if what I'm about to tell you should really come as any surprise. But before I tell you the rest of June's story, let me give you a bit more background. I don't want to force the climax, after all. The area where June had her store was one of those little neighborhoods in a big city that is simply overrun with babies and toddlers. It seemed that only youngish couples lived there, and that each youngish couple had one kid exactly— somewhere between the ages of three-and-a-half months and four years old. And so this little neighborhood was full of the intense love and care and devotion that first time parents harbor. And on any given day, rain or shine, the sidewalks of this little neighborhood were simply teeming with babies and toddlers (and the doleful parents who loved them). And there was the gear, of course —the crisp, vaguely trendy diaper bags; the blazingly white burp cloths; the strollers designed by NASA. And all of it, naturally, could be found in June's little store.

Anyway, should it come as any surprise when one morning, just as June was done tending to the cash drawer and she was about to open up the store for the day, she saw them gathered there outside her front windows? They were gathered there with their tiny fists and their fish lips—so sweet—pressed right up against the plate glass. Not a parent in sight, mind you. For June, this was not a sweet scene. She didn't move from behind the little counter. There was nothing that she could do but stand there and watch the crowd of them grow and grow, multiplying right outside her store. One or two of them must have sent out a secret signal, some piercing laugh/squeal that only they can hear. And they kept coming. Because they had figured her out.

June loved helping her customers find that perfect gift for a friend who was expecting or a niece's first birthday. She truly did. She would write long notes of congratulations (by hand) for the nervous first time mothers who had spent hours upon hours in her shop during their pregnancies, crying over the endless piles of tiny booties and bibs. When those mothers had their babies, she would send a note to the hospital room, tied around the neck of one of the tiny, slightly scratchy owl rattles made of brightly dyed, hand-spun wool. The welts that must have risen on the fists and cheeks of those poor newborn babes, but those owls were so damn precious.

But as I was saying, on a bright, ordinary morning, a massive crowd of babies and toddlers gathered outside of June's shop. And though they were small and smiling and drooling, the force of all of them together there, pushing up against the plate glass of her shop windows, was actually quite disturbing. Frightening, in fact. Nothing about the scene was heartbreaking or sweet. Not the little, bowed legs or the tiny, pink fists. Not even how they reached out for each other's cheeks and eyes with that wet, open-mouthed curiosity that all babies have. June stood there behind the little counter and understood that this was not good. She stood there and thought about how glad she was that the shop door was still locked. Although her hate had not been something that she had directly pondered much over the years, the scene outside her shop somehow made sense to her. And yes, she was scared. Like I said, these babies—who were now beginning to pound on the plate glass—had figured June out. It wasn't hard. They had peeled back that perfectly imperfect wrapping job of hers and discovered what was sitting there, just inside.

hank

My mother is appalled.

"Who would name their baby Hank?" she asks me over the phone. "I mean—Hank. Don't you think that will be weird?" she asks me, "babysitting a baby named Hank?"

"I don't know," I tell her. "I haven't even met the family yet."

"Hank." My mother says it again.

I've got tears in my eyes. She makes me laugh.

"Who would name their baby Hank?" She is desperate to know.

When I meet Jane, she is full of nervous first-time-mom chatter. Is it weird, she wants to know, that she saw my flyer at the down-town YMCA and then called me, a complete stranger, and asked me to meet her child? I assure her that I don't think it's weird.

"It's a great way to find babysitting jobs," I tell her.

"That's what I was thinking," she says, feathering her dark hair with her fingers and biting her lower lip. Her smiles are fast and spectacular. Her teeth are perfectly small and white.

"I've got quite a few references," I tell her. "I've been baby-sitting for the past two years that I've been in grad school." I hand her a list of names and phone numbers.

"And it's not weird for me to call these people and talk to them for a bit," Jane says.

I'm not sure what to say, because she hasn't stated this as a question, yet she sounds so unsure.

"Definitely not weird," I say.

Jane smiles.

She shows me around the house. And this is always the most fascinating part. Seeing someone's pantry for the first time is like visiting a foreign country. And no two families keep their extra toilet paper in the same place. Some families leave their under-wear out in piles on top of the dryer—sometimes folded, some-times not—and others don't. I once babysat for a family with five kids and the mom insisted that they all did their laundry to-gether on Sundays. I'd wake up late on Sunday morning and im-agine the Martins in their basement, all seven of them curled up with books and magazines and a deck of Uno in front of the whirl of the washer and dryer. Jane's house is clean. The paper towels are where they should be and the bathroom shines. She shows me the master bedroom. The books on the night table are in a perfect stack. The bed is tightly made with one silk corner pulled down for show. Jane smiles and seems to enjoy my praise.

"Just our little home," she says.

It's huge.

She opens their closet to show me just how far you can walk in. Her husband's stiff blazers brush against my shoulder. Jane's pointed shoes stand at attention, lined up in tight rows. Jane hasn't shown me Hank's room. He must be sleeping.

"Hank's asleep?" I ask.

Jane jumps a bit at the question, and I can tell she might not quite be ready for me to meet him yet. She's scared, really. I am, after all, the first babysitter. Jane leads me into the nursery, and I hear the tinkle of baby music and see the orange glow of night-lights and baby monitors. The smell is sweet powder and warm milk. Jane watches Hank for several moments. She pulls the thin, blue blanket up over the small bulk of his body and shoots me one of her spectacular smiles as if to say, "See, this must be the best I can do." And then she says, "Hank," aloud. "This is Hank," she says softly as the two of us peer down at the sleeping baby. The name seems perfectly fine trailing out of a mother's mouth.

HANK says, "My name's Hank," when I babysit for the first time a few days later. He says it the exact moment when we are left alone together: "My name's Hank." And I say, "I know." Then I realize, holding him in my arms, that I am speaking with a five-month-old. My breath catches. We're sitting at the kitchen table. Hank looks up at me and tells me how he likes it when Jane watches him sleep, like when I saw him for the first time a couple days ago. "Sometimes I'm awake when she watches me," he says. He tells me how he feigns sleep and tries not to smile. "I know she can be such a worried bird sometimes," Hank says, "but I love it when she watches me. I don't mind."

Hank looks up at me again. We watch each other.

"You're talking to me," I say.

JANE and I soon become good friends—in the way that babysitters and nervous, thin, first-time mothers can. She trusts me with her baby. She likes me as a person. I'm young! I'm fun! I'm free on weeknights! Jane's husband, Paul, is quiet. He works a lot. When he's home, he usually shuts himself up in his deep, mahogany study. I caught a glimpse once when Paul wasn't home. It was dark, and all I saw were blinking lights and the shadows cast by huge, metallic-looking shelves. It looks like the CIA in there. When Paul comes home from work or out from his study, he grabs at Hank and twirls the baby in his arms somewhat awkwardly. "This is my son," he wants to tell me. He's shy.

It is hard for Hank and me to get to know each other at first. Jane hangs around a great deal during the first several times I babysit in order to "get things done around the house." She wants to be there, I know, in case I forget where the extra burpy cloths are kept. She wants to be there in the event that I don't remember how to work the DVD player, because then there would be no Baby Mozart. It's hard to murmur about the weather (it's been raining nonstop for four days), let alone really talk with Jane constantly charging in mid-chore with her smiles and a hug for baby. "It's weird talking with you like this with her just in the other room," I tell Hank. He tells me we're quiet enough, and he asks me to carry him into the kitchen so he can show me Jane's miniature herb garden on the windowsill above the sink. Hank asks me to hold each tiny pot up to his face.

"I love these smells," he tells me. "I like it when she cooks and uses these. You can smell it all over the house." Hank sniffs. "Especially this one."

"It's basil," I say.

I'm not sure how to describe Hank's voice. It's quiet, yet full. It's not high and it's not low. It's the voice you hear when you think of a child, I guess.

I notice a note on the counter. It is written in tight, blocky script:

"Jane," it says, "The dry-cleaning—my shirts."

When I babysit a lot for one family I can't help but speculate. Who wouldn't? I've met parents who have everything together. Parents who chart-out carpools on the refrigerator and still manage to get out together and have fun. They come home late at night buzzing and stand in the living room with me for a bit to talk. When their arms brush, it seems electric. I've also met parents who are surprised at the fact that they are parents.

And parents who parent too much and seem to forget about the husband and wife part. I touch the note on the counter and think of Paul and Jane. I think of how rigid Jane's back was the other night when Paul came home and asked her for a kiss. I think of how Paul sometimes narrows his eyes when he hears Jane's voice.

"Want to sit on the porch swing out front?" Hank asks me.

"Sure," I say, and we watch the steady rain for the rest of the slow afternoon.

JOSHUA, the guy I've been seeing, asks if he can come with me sometime when I babysit. I tell him I don't think so. "Jane's kind of weird about things like that," I tell him. Jane has actually asked me about Joshua quite a few times. "I want to meet your boyfriend," she tells me, and her voice lowers with the final word as if we are sharing a delicate secret. I'm not quite sure yet what to think of the whole situation—a talking baby, that is, who's becoming a good friend. I'm not sure that I'm ready to take Joshua with me to Hank's house.

Joshua asks what I do when I have to spend hours with a baby.

"Is it boring?" he asks. He kisses my finger and I wonder if he somehow thinks it's romantic—me with a baby.

"It's not boring," I say. "Hank's one of the best babies I've ever babysat for."

"Why?"

"I don't know," I say, pulling at his earlobe, "He's just easy-going, I guess."

"Hank's a weird name."

"My mom thinks so, too."

"What does a Hank look like?" Joshua asks.

Hank's still almost completely bald, even at five-and-a-half months. He's puffy and soft and he's got big, blue eyes.

"Hard to describe," I say.

I wonder if I can say that Joshua is my boyfriend; it's only been two and a half months. I inadvertently locked our bikes together outside the public library, and that's how we met. I don't tell many people this, because I can tell that they think it's too cute. And it is. Joshua doesn't have long legs, but they sort of gallop when he walks. And I like that.

I ASK Hank if it gets lonely, talking only with me.

"It's not like that," he says.

We are baking cookies. It's a surprise for Jane. She is hosting her first Candle Party today at her house. The dim glow of at least a dozen expensive candles can be seen at the bottom of the door that separates the kitchen from the living room, where Jane's female acquaintances are sipping dry wine. The low murmur of their voices is occasionally punctuated by Jane's enthusiastic laugh. Jane stopped working when she became pregnant with Hank. She used to be a personal buyer. Women would hire her to manage their wardrobes. I imagine Jane pacing the huge closets of wealthy women and smiling and saying what great tastes and figures they have while calculating in her head what shoes and blazers and slips she would buy. Jane tells me she's not ready to go back to work yet, but that she misses it. That's why she's decided to host expensive Candle Parties for her friends. It's new and it's risky, quite a big investment. Jane likes it that way.

I hold Hank above the bowl of thick batter and he drops the heavy spoon on the floor. His fists are still too weak.

"Babies grow so fast," I say.

I have only been babysitting Hank for a few weeks, and already I can feel how his body has grown heavier when I pull him up to me from out of his crib or the baby swing.

"Does time go by fast for you?" Hank asks me. He looks up at me and I notice the tiny, raised milk bumps on his forehead.

"I think so," I say. "How about you?"

"I don't think it does," Hank says.

I hold him close to the bowl of batter and let him slap the tough dough with his palms. His eyes are wide. I can tell it's like nothing he's ever felt before. His giggles are full of air.

JANE is only a little nervous the first time she asks me to bathe Hank. She loves me. She loves the way I'm not afraid to make exclamatory and enthusiastic baby sounds when she's in the same room. She loves how naturally Hank and I get along. I swing him into the air and he acts surprised, trying to suppress gurgles. Usually Jane bathes Hank in the morning. But she didn't have time today and now she's in a rush to meet Paul for dinner. "It's a business arrangement," she tells me. She's anxious and she asks me to zip up her thin, black dress in the living room. Her back is smooth and delicate, like a flat, glossy table. Jane's always a wreck when she has to make an appearance at any of Paul's work events. I know she's worried about what people will think of her, even about what Paul will think. "Take this," she says, untying the red silk scarf that is around her neck and handing it to me. "Have it," she says, "It's yours." Jane's always giving me clothes, especially when she's nervous. She'll peel something off in disgust and throw it at me, ordering me to keep it. She hurled one of her bras at me once. "Ridiculous," she said, flinging it to me from where it lay crumpled on the bed. The bra was black, expensive and lacy. I didn't keep it. It would have been too small. Even if it did fit, I could never imagine actually wearing one of Jane's bras. I fasten the hook at the top of Jane's slim dress and Hank watches from his corner. He's started to crawl and has told me that he spends a lot of time in the playpen when I'm not there. He calls it "the cage" to make me laugh.

Jane asks me how she looks and I say, "Stunning," and she makes me say it again before she slides out the front door. Jane has told me how happy she is that Hank isn't yet in that heartbreaking baby stage where they always cry when Mommy leaves.

"I won't sink," Hank tells me.

"Not a chance," I say.

Jane still insists on bathing Hank in the kitchen sink. She thinks it's "charming and delightful" to have a baby in the sink. It's a large kitchen sink and the smooth folds of Hank's body still fit with plenty of room to spare in the beautiful brushed-steel basin, but I think it's weird and wish I had taken him upstairs to the bathtub.

"Just let go of me for a second," Hank says. "I could float."

The water is warm and soft with Baby Magic. I can smell the herbs on the windowsill.

"I'm not going to let go of you."

"Just let me try."

The water isn't at all deep. It barely hits Hank's ribs as I hold him up in a sitting position and buff his bald head with a soft, damp cloth.

"Let me try," he says again.

I let go of Hank's slick body and he smiles, clear baby drool rushing down his dimple chin. He leans back and he does float, maybe for a second or two. But then he starts to panic and the water reaches for the curve of his neck, his small chin, his nose and his mouth. It happens quickly. Hank lets out a cry, a baby cry that I've never heard from him before. The big kitchen echoes with his cry. I am swift, and in a moment we are sitting together in the living room. Hank is speechless in my arms, wrapped in only a towel with a bottle to his lips.

WHEN Joshua sees me on campus, or on the corner of my street, he trips over his feet in an attempt to get to me as quickly as possible. We're in that awkward, good phase. He often repeats my name incessantly. When we're lying together, he tries to grasp all of my thick hair in only one of his fists. Things with Joshua are going well. I tell Hank this while feeding him one afternoon, and he insists that I bring Joshua with me sometime.

"You sure?" I ask.

"I want to see him," he says.

Hank's in his highchair. I'm feeding him spoonfuls of mashed squash. He's making the slow transition to solid foods. We've been discussing astronomy. Hank often asks me to carry him out into the middle of the wide backyard when I am babysitting late at night. I took an introductory astronomy course in college, and he makes me repeat what I know over and over. He says the name of each constellation after I say it. I often feel guilty because of how excited Hank gets when I point to a cluster of stars. I didn't do well in astronomy, and sometimes I'll just point at anything and say what it is even though I have no idea if that's what it is—just to please Hank. I don't think Hank's caught on. He'll wave his hand in the direction I've pointed and stare up into the dotted sky.

"You should take another astronomy class," Hank says as I offer him another spoonful of squash.

"You do my homework," I say, sliding the spoon into his tiny mouth.

"Really, Maria," he has already swallowed, "I think you should."

Hank's face suddenly relaxes. He stares past my shoulder and smiles like a maniac, his cheeks and lips covered in shiny squash. I hear the key in the back door and realize that it's Jane. She bursts into the kitchen with smiles for both baby and me.

JANE pulls me into her bedroom when I bring Joshua with me that next Saturday night.

"I like him," she says in a low voice. She winks. Her eyes are huge and smoky with makeup. I breathe in her peppery perfume. The whole room is saturated.

"You think?" I ask.

"Maria, I like him," she says. "It makes me excited to spend a night out with Paul, just the two of us."

It was hard to believe that either Jane or Paul was excited when Joshua and I first arrived. I think we walked into the staleness of an incomplete argument, of things left unsaid.

"And look at my stomach," Jane tells me, "Do you think I'm trimming down?" Jane pulls her silk blouse tight against her ribs. "Does my stomach look flat in this?"

The edge of her shirt rises a bit as she stretches it across her front. I catch a glimpse of her firm belly and see the tail end of a quick, pink scar. I wonder if it's a scar from having Hank.

"You look really good," I tell Jane.

"Yeah?"

"Yeah."

Paul laughs downstairs. Jane grabs my hand and the two of us descend the steps and walk into the living room. I feel like I'm presenting royalty. Jane makes me feel that way. Joshua and Paul stand together above Hank's playpen. They are taking turns trying to bounce a Nerf ball off of Hank's big head. Joshua's idea, I'm sure. Paul is dressed in a dark suit and he smells like clean laundry. Joshua is a full head shorter and he's wearing a thin Batman T-shirt with a hole at the collar. "Watch this, Maria," he says, and the Nerf ball rebounds off of Hank's head. Hank loves it. He screams with throaty, shrill laughter the way delighted babies do.

"Joshua, he loves you," Jane says. Hank laughs again and Jane exclaims, "Fun, Fun, Fun!" She runs across the room to where the ball has landed, her thin heels piercing the thick carpet. Paul's face sags a bit. I can tell he wants to roll his eyes. Jane throws the ball to Joshua and links her arm through her husband's.

"A night out," she says.

Paul doesn't say anything.

Joshua and I order a pizza and let Hank loose from the play-pen. He's been crawling like mad lately. "It's almost like floating at first," Hank told me last week, "You don't remember that?" Hank sidles over to where we are sitting on the floor. He pulls himself up using the edge of the coffee table and emits a baby "Huffff."

"I'm going to put him to bed," I say.

Joshua pokes Hank's big belly. "Later, man."

When we are upstairs in his room, I ask Hank: "What do you think your first word will be?"

I snap up his pajamas.

"I don't know," he says.

I stand Hank up on the changing table, and he holds my two index fingers in his hands. His legs are strong. He's getting taller.

"Do you want me to rock you?" I ask.

"No."

When I babysit at night, Hank and I often stay up until Paul and Jane get home. Sometimes I don't even put him in his crib. We watch TV or just talk. Sometimes we take ourselves on tours of the quiet house. We creep into the huge basement or climb up into the clean, cedar attic. We explore places Hank hasn't seen yet: the walk-in shower in Paul and Jane's bedroom, the linen closet on the third floor, the tool shed that looks like a small barn in the backyard. Everything is vast and clean. Sometimes we walk a few paces into Paul's study, but I never turn on the lights and we don't stay that long. We just listen to the buzz of the room for a moment and then back out. I never feel like I'm snooping because Hank's with me and he lives there. We're always back on the couch by the time Paul and Jane get home. At first I thought it might upset Jane that I didn't always follow her bedtime routine. But she thinks it's charming to come home late at night with drink on her breath and find me curled up on the couch reading or watching TV with Hank supposedly asleep in my arms.

Hank looks up at me from where I've placed him in his crib.

"I like Joshua," he says.

"He threw a ball at your head."

"I know."

I'll admit it is awkward, some of these moments with Hank. Like putting him to bed now. If he were a little boy, six or seven years old, everything would fit. Our conversations might make sense. I run my thumb over his silk eyebrow.

"I'll see you in a couple of days," I say.

"Maria?" Hank asks.

"Yeah?"

I'm standing at his door, about to leave it open a crack.

"I don't think Paul and Jane love each other anymore."

For some reason, I'm not surprised to hear Hank refer to his parents by their first names. If Hank were older, what would I say?

"Do you want to talk about it?" I come back to his crib.

"Do you think I'm right?"

"You could be," I say.

I'm not surprised that Hank has noticed something that even I have picked up on.

"They're my parents." Hank says this as if it's an idea he's simply curious about.

"And you're their baby."

It's sad, I want to say, Isn't it sad?

"Do you want me to rock you?" I ask again.

"No. Goodnight."

Hank finds a pacifier in the folds of his blanket and places it in his mouth. He doesn't want to talk any more tonight.

Joshua is asleep when I come back downstairs. He's stretched out on the carpet, breathing loudly. I try to envision Jane roaming the big rooms in the middle of the afternoon with her vacuum. I see Paul in his suit at the end of a long day making a thin sandwich at the kitchen counter. And then there's Hank: in his highchair, or beside the big couch, or standing in a corner of the playpen with his hands reaching up over the top and his face pressed into the thin, white mesh. Most of the lights in the house are off and the flickering colors of the quiet TV mix with shadows on the living room walls. The walls of the house are covered with photographs of Hank as well as photographs of Paul and Jane. Paul and Jane dancing on their wedding day. Paul and Jane golfing. Paul and Jane carving a huge pumpkin. Paul and Jane sipping wine on their honeymoon, their arms tangled. I wish that the photographs were tiny, moving pictures so I could watch the two of them smiling and laughing then.

I lie down on the floor facing Joshua. "Hey," he says and kisses me. He pushes me gently on the shoulder, kisses me again.

"No," I say.

"I know," he says, "You're the babysitter. That's gross."

"I know," I laugh.

We shift our bodies closer to one another on the thick carpet. We kiss as softly as we can. I laugh the entire time. We're making out, I keep thinking to myself. I'm making out while babysitting.

We sit up when we hear Paul and Jane at the front door and pretend to watch an episode of *Seinfeld*. I swear Jane notices the few strands of hair that have been pulled out of my tight ponytail. She smiles at me before she says goodnight and goes upstairs. Paul sits in the living room with us for a while and talks with Joshua about fishing. He tells us how he can't wait to take Hank out on a lake for the first time. He raises his hands up off of his lap when he says this, and his smile is huge.

JANE is out hosting a Candle Party at another woman's house when I arrive to babysit a few days later. Paul meets me in the driveway. He's been walking Hank in his jogging stroller, and he's dressed for work.

"We named him after my grandfather." Paul pushes the stroller toward me. Hank and I look at each other.

"It's a good name," I say.

"That's what I think." Paul picks Hank up and hugs him, rubbing his back. I'm always amazed at how babies fold into adult bodies.

"Jane said you guys should walk to the zoo today."

"Good idea," I say, and Paul hands me Hank. He pretends to steal Hank's nose and makes a big show of it. Hank just looks at him with wide eyes and doesn't laugh.

Paul drives away slowly and waves to Hank and me before turning away from us and onto a different street.

It is the middle of fall, my favorite time of year, and Hank's stroller rolls smoothly over the dry leaves. He hasn't said anything about what we talked about on Saturday night when I put him to bed. I don't want to talk about it either. Hank doesn't say much because most of the sidewalks are congested with people once we get closer to the zoo. He fumbles with the zipper of his jacket, sucking on it and trying to eat it the way babies try to eat everything that feels hard and cool against their swollen, broken gums.

When we get to the zoo, I push his stroller right up against the glass of the huge aquarium and watch him watch the fish. There are three other strollers lined up next to Hank's. All four babies stare into the liquid blue, their mouths slightly open.

"What do you think, Hank?" I ask.

Hank turns in his stroller and looks back at me when he hears his name. He sucks in air and puckers his lips and then turns back to the thick glass.

The gorilla is huge. A zoo tour guide stops next to Hank and me and tells the group of elementary students that she is leading about the gorilla. It's a male, and he was born in captivity. Hank and I watch him. He's sitting in the grass near the edge of a cliff with a moat of water far below him, which is supposed to keep him from escaping and joining us outside his exhibit.

"He has escaped before," the tour guide says, and I see the eyes of the elementary kids grow wide. "But now there's deep water down there and he won't try it again," she adds, and the children relax a bit.

I try to imagine the escape and wonder if it was a big affair —fangs bared, huge hands splayed and all that. I picture the gorilla running through city streets and cutting through backyards, crushing swing sets. People watching him through small bathroom windows. The tour guide says he was confused and dazed and that he simply hid in the women's restroom.

"We shot him with tranquilizers," she says, "to make him sleepy."

She tells the group that the gorilla is now being treated for depression. Hank turns in his stroller and looks up at me. "I know," I want to say, "That's weird." How do you treat a huge gorilla for depression? You can't just sit him in a comfortable chair and untangle his childhood and his mother. I want to tell Hank later, as we are walking home, that it must be drugs. Maybe shots, or an I.V. while he sleeps. I picture the setup—slow drops falling into him while he snores. We all watch the gorilla and wonder if he's sad. He watches us back in furtive glimpses. He actually sighs with each quick glance. And it's so human-like, those sighs. He picks tiny blades of grass and delicately twirls them between his huge, black fingers. He sticks one in his mouth and lightly sucks it. He looks up and sighs.

"He was born in captivity," the guide says again. Perhaps she senses our sadness. "He wouldn't survive out in the jungle," she tells the children.

And I agree. He probably wouldn't make it wading through all that green. The gorilla sits hunched like a fat Buddha in the grass. The last of the day's sun nests in his thick fur. He shyly watches us watch him, and I try to catch what interests him most. Eventually I notice that it's the children whom he's curious about. Their cries and laughs are what attract his longest stares. I think I see him watch silent, little Hank for a moment or two.

It is dusk when Hank and I get back to the house. Jane and Paul are in the kitchen when we come in through the back door. It's apparent that Hank and I have walked into the middle of something. The air is thick with nothing being said. Jane's face is flushed and Paul's face is white. They are sitting across from each other at the kitchen table but not exactly facing one another. Jane has a butter knife in her hand and she tries to twirl it lightly like a baton, but her hand is too fast and shaky. Paul gets up and leaves the room, keeping an eye on the tile floor as he walks out. Something sparks and Jane is suddenly full of exciting questions for Hank. She lifts him high into the air and says, "Did you see the animals, Pumpkin? Did you see any giraffes?" We hear a door shut somewhere upstairs. Jane seems practically out of breath and her voice rises as she lifts Hank even higher, toward the ceiling. "Any monkeys?" she chirps, and Hank looks down and laughs for her.

"Maria, I've got a favor to ask," Jane says.

She sets Hank in his highchair and begins to take off his jacket. I wonder if she's going to ask me to stay tonight. I'm supposed to meet Joshua for dinner in an hour. He's made reservations at an expensive Japanese place downtown where they cook your food right in front of you on your table. I've never been.

"I need a partner for my yoga class tonight," Jane says. "I forgot tonight was Partner Yoga night and Paul can't go. He's got to get some things done for work. You know," she says, "get some things done here at home."

Hank grabs a handful of Jane's black hair. She kisses his hand before gently pulling herself free.

"So, what do you think?" Jane turns to me. She smiles but her face is flat. Paul has stood her up, I can see. He doesn't want to go to her stupid Partner Yoga class. My stomach sinks at the thought of not seeing Joshua tonight. Hank watches me.

"I've got to call Joshua and let him know," I say.

"Oh! If you've got plans."

"No, I can go, Jane. It's not a big deal. It will be fun," I say. "Yoga, huh?"

"Yeah, ever done it?"

"No."

I leave Jane and Hank in the kitchen and call Joshua from the living room. He's disappointed.

"Partner Yoga?" he asks.

"Yeah, Partner Yoga. I feel bad. Paul can't go. She needs this to relax," I say. "First time mom and all that stuff."

"Teach me some moves later?"

"Definitely."

Joshua laughs.

"I don't want to go to yoga tonight," Jane announces as she backs her car out of their driveway.

"You don't?"

"No. But I do want to be out of the house," she says, "and you're good company." Jane guns the gas. She's giddy with escape.

"Okay," I say. "Where to?"

"A bar," Jane says. "I want a drink."

Both Jane and I are soon drunk. For two hours we dine only on stale peanuts while drinking beer, then vodka martinis. It's the first time I've had them and the dry, fire taste scorches my mouth. I can't decide if I like it, so I keep drinking. Everything we talk about is strange and surreal because we're drunk and we'd never expect this, the two of us together in a musty downtown bar. We love it.

"Have you and Joshua had sex?" Jane asks me. Her lips are wet from her martini.

"That's a stupid question," I say.

"Why?"

"Because you asked it," I say. "Because I won't answer it."

Joshua and I are constantly fumbling at each other's clothes. We pull at one another by shirtsleeves and even pant zippers to get each other's attention, even when we're in public. I imagine wearing the tiny, lace bra that Jane tried to give me, Joshua slowly unbuttoning my shirt. The tiny bra would have rubbed and left deep, itchy, beautiful patterns on my skin. I can tell that my smile makes Jane think that Joshua and I have had sex, but we haven't yet. I look at her. Jane is beautiful. She's not chirpy mom and she's not chirpy wife and she's not even chirpy Jane. She's just dark, flushed, drunk Jane. And I'm drunk Maria, flushed and beautiful too, I hope.

I realize how drunk we are when we rise from our unsteady barstools and fumble across the street to a fancy French restaurant, one of Jane's favorites. "I'm craving snails," Jane says and we head straight for the ladies room in the back of the restaurant where we pee in neighboring stalls for at least a minute straight, laughing. Jane orders escargot and melted cheeses and bread. Everything is delicious. I manage to pretend that I'm not eating snails. I catch the price of the bottle of red wine that Jane orders on the wine list and I'm breathless. The waiter knows we're drunk. He fills our glasses with wine and makes us feel like we belong, a young mother and her son's babysitter sitting conspiratorially close in a dark, expensive restaurant.

"So you and Joshua have done it," Jane says.

"Shut up." I use one of the snails as a puppet.

"Paul and I have done it."

"Shut up, Jane." This time, two snails.

"Paul's an asshole," Jane announces. She seems to sober up a bit when she says it.

"Paul's an asshole," I repeat. Then, "Paul's an asshole?" I feel like I should make it into a question.

There are three bowls of different melted cheeses between us. Jane holds a hunk of bread above them.

"What do you think I should do?" Jane asks me.

I pretend that she's asking about the cheeses. Jane waits for me to answer while she holds her bread up in the air.

"I can't tell you what to do," I tell Jane.

We call Joshua when we get outside and ask him to come pick us up.

"Where are you?" Joshua wants to know, "What time is it?"

"It is two in the morning and we are at Don's downtown. You know Don's?"

"Don's?"

"Don's."

Joshua wakes up a bit. "I know Don's," he says.

He's in sweatpants that are too small for him and his hair is flat against his head when he comes to pick us up.

"You're adorable," Jane says.

She falls asleep in the backseat right away and snores delicately. I hold Joshua's hand as he drives her home. He keeps looking over at me, his eyes bright. He's confused. I kiss his hand. Joshua asks me what happened tonight, and I whisper, "All I know is that Paul's an asshole. That's all I've been told." My head spins from sitting in the car.

"I'm sorry we didn't have Japanese," I say. I need to ground myself with my own voice.

Joshua tells me again how they cook the food right there on your table.

"The chefs are these big guys in white, and they try to tell stupid jokes," he says.

I wake Jane when we get to her house and she insists that we come in with her and check on Hank.

"Okay," I say.

Joshua looks at me sideways.

"Wait!" Jane says.

She points at the moon. Joshua and I follow her into the backyard. The moon is full and high. It sits far above their back fence like a hanging silver bulb.

"I want to show Hank the moon," I say.

"Let's go get him," Jane says, and Joshua finally lets himself laugh out loud.

The inside of the house is dark. The three of us feel our way using walls and the backs of couches. Jane leads us up the cool, marble stairs. She presses Hank's door lightly with her palm and it opens. The glow of the nightlight illuminates us enough to see one another. Joshua grabs my hand.

"Hank," Jane whispers.

She un-tucks the edges of Hank's blanket from under his sides. She touches his thumb with her own. I wonder if the room smells like red wine, if that's possible.

"Hank." Jane says it louder.

He opens his eyes. Jane and I both look down at him. He's surprised. He's silent.

"Hold him, Maria," Jane says.

I hold Hank and watch as he fights to wake up. He rotates his head lazily around the room and seems to count the people. He looks at me. His pajamas are soft and warm against my bare arms. Jane stands away from Hank and watches him take everything in.

We go back out into the backyard and Jane points to the moon. She says "moon" over and over in Hank's ear and points up into the sky. Hank sees it. He reaches his hand out and Jane jumps up and down. "He's trying to touch it," she says. "He's reaching out like he could touch it."

The four of us watch the moon.

"Do you guys know how I had him?" Jane asks.

Joshua and I don't say anything.

"Jane?" Paul stands at the back door. His voice is dry. He's in large, plaid pajamas that hang loosely from him. He looks around and doesn't seem shocked to see the four of us standing in his backyard in the middle of the night. Paul joins us out on the lawn. Our ankles are lost in the tall grass.

"Jane's drunk," Paul says. He brushes Jane's arm with his index finger. He starts to wake up.

"Maria's drunk," I say.

"I'm not," Joshua says. "I gave them a ride home." Joshua shrugs for Paul, and Paul shrugs back.

"Do you want to know how I had him?" Jane asks again.

"Jane," Paul says, "You're drunk. Where's the car?"

"Paul, let's be reasonable," she says. Her voice is soft and harsh at the same time. "Let's be reasonable." Jane says it again. She turns back to us. "It was pretty normal, I guess," she says. "But it was having a baby. That's big. It's a big deal for anyone. And they had to take him out," she says. "They had to just take him out."

Paul smooths her hair back, and it's a strange thing to see. It's not a lovely touch. It's not an intimate touch. He just smooths her hair back and then goes back into the house. The kitchen bursts with yellow light. The four of us look up at the moon again. Joshua gives me his jacket and I wrap it around Hank like a blanket. He chews on one of the buttons. I sway lightly with Hank on my hip, like we're dancing. Nobody says anything until Paul comes back outside with a glass in each hand. I hear the chink of ice cubes and guess it's something like scotch.

"You and I should have a drink," Paul says to Joshua as he hands him a glass. Paul nods at Jane and me. "We should catch up."

Joshua winces after his first sip. He looks at Paul. They clink their glasses.

Jane watches Paul drink. He takes a bunch of little sips and then one long pull.

"Paul, what do you remember?" she asks.

"Jane," he says.

She turns to Joshua and me and watches Hank bobbing in my arms. I remember the tip of her pink scar, like tiny train tracks. Jane takes Hank from me. The ghost of his weight remains in my arms. She kisses his head. She kisses his hand. "Hank," she says, and her voice splits. Jane takes him over to Paul. She lifts Hank up high and weaves him through the air in front of his father. Hank starts to cry. It's the sharp, baby cry I heard the first time I gave him a bath. I want to ask him what he remembers, if he remembers anything. I want to ask him the next time we are alone together. He's got to tell me. Hank's cry pierces the still night. Paul starts to take the baby from Jane, but she won't let him. She says something real quiet, and then Paul says, "You're drunk, Jane." Jane hands the baby to her husband. Paul's cold drink rests against Hank's back. Jane presses herself into Paul's side and it's an uneasy movement, a tick. We all keep standing and glancing at the sky. Hank keeps crying.

"Everyone's crying," Joshua whispers, nudging me. I look at Paul standing under the moon with his son in his arms, and I do think I see tears. But it's hard to tell because the glow of the moon is so weak. I watch Paul. He bobs Hank like I had, and a little bit of his drink splashes onto Hank's back. He says, "Shhhhh," and tries to smile, like this is all so silly. I wonder if he's crying, and I think, What if Paul leaves? What if he leaves for good? I see boxes piled up in the living room. I see Hank taking his first, shaky steps within a tight row of boxes labeled, "Study." Joshua and I watch the three of them and don't know what to do. Their bodies are joined by shadow, one soft, large mass. Hank's in the middle of two people I really don't know. He's a piece of both of them, such a little piece. He was born. The three of them share that one event—the blood and the tightening of muscles, the letting go.

Hank won't look at me. His face is buried in Paul's neck. He tries to catch quick, staccato breaths in between cries. It's like nothing I've ever heard, and I want to tell him that.

the rockport falls retirement
village rescuers

I STARE AT the scatter of groceries all around me on the dull linoleum. The can of baked beans is dented, and I have to stop myself from groaning aloud about that. I close my eyes and try to center myself on the rescue, envisioning it as they have taught us to do. I listen for Nora's footsteps, her timid knock on the door before she takes the spare key to my apartment from around her thin neck and turns it in the lock. I can't get over how stupid I feel.

Nora and I were paired up during Rescuer Orientation here at Rockport Falls Retirement Village when we were both new tenants. We went through the rigorous three-week program and then received the little metal tags that exclaim: "Rockport Falls Retirement Village Rescuer!" which we wear around our necks, along with the spare keys to each other's apartments. Nora and I have been saving each other after bad falls (they actually prefer that we use the term *rescue*) for just under a year now. She's slipped while getting out of the bathtub a couple times. I've tripped over the vacuum cleaner cord and rolled out of bed in the middle of the night. And now this, my groceries all over the kitchen floor. I don't even know how it happened this time.

Does anything hurt? Nora asks after letting herself in. She peers in at me from the little entryway to my apartment, afraid of what she might see. I shake my head, and she inches in closer. This is usually the first thing we ask each other, about the pain. I guess this is because pain is one of the most common experiences that binds all of us together as we race toward the ends of our lives here at the Village. And so we measure ourselves against each other in this way, openly and unabashedly pouring over the details of our aching hips and our tender gums and our spastic, stuttering hearts. Nothing hurts, I tell her. I can tell that nothing is broken. Maybe I could even pull myself up off of the kitchen floor unassisted. But I'm too mortified to try. Nora steps over the dented can of baked beans and doesn't bend down right away, because it takes a lot of courage to crouch down at our age and know that you are going to have to get yourself back up again.

The training during Rescuer Orientation is intense. Nora and I were set up at our own card table in the cafeteria for four hours each afternoon, left alone to quiz each other from the workbook and get used to staring into each other's eyes for ten minute stretches. It was so awkward, especially those first few days. Nora and I had never met before coming to the Village, and now we were expected to learn how to navigate each other's souls. Because this is how the rescues work. It's like telepathy, I guess, although the instructors never used that exact term. They continuously talked about the soul, throwing around phrases like *soul sight* and *soul seeing* and *soul searching*. All of us new tenants thought it was such a joke, of course. But the Rescuer Program has allowed the administration to make pretty significant cuts in the number of people on their staff, creating funding for more perks for the residents. The amenities at Rockport Falls Retirement Village are top-notch. The wait list is one of the longest in the region. Of course we put up with all the hoops they made us jump through during training, snickering about it together over lunch and Bridge. We snickered, even after we all began to feel it working. Even after the first out of our group of new residents tripped over his own two feet and was saved by his partner.

Sorry it took so long, Nora says, readying herself to bend down. It took no time at all, I say. I wiggle my fingers. I wiggle my toes. I'm perfectly fine. I was sitting in front of one of my shows on TV, Nora says. I got confused for a minute there, she says. About if you were calling me in for a rescue or if it was just some of the drama and gobblideegook on the show. It was me, I say. And here I am, she says.

They group the new residents together into same-sex pairs. Because you'd be surprised at the amount of flirting and drama that breeds and multiplies in a place like the Village. So many of us have lost our husbands and our wives, and I'm afraid that we act like teenagers. Plain and simple. The old Baptist preacher who lives down the hall is senile and in love with both Nora and me. He fell for Nora first. During the long days of training, he'd sidle up to our card table while she and I were trying to get used to looking each other in the eye and she'd swat him away without blinking once. Then he cornered me in the hall a few weeks later and called me sweetheart and honey and leaned against my door with his frail, saggy shoulder expecting to be let in. I swatted him away, just like Nora. I even gave him a little shove for good measure. For some reason, I can't bring myself to tell Nora about it. So what if an old, senile widower has professed his love for both of us (and probably since forgotten)? After all the rescues that Nora and I have already done for each other, we've been forced to become intimate and close. When you are looking into someone else's eyes, really searching and waiting for that strange strength to surge through your limbs like electric jelly, you get tuned into a certain frequency and you can't help but pick up on

some of the things that are tucked into what the Rescuer Orientation instructors call the white noise. There are things about
Nora that I know now because I've seen them in brilliant flashes,
just behind her dim pupils. Her mother's hands, for instance.
Her favorite doll. The little, light-filled sunporch tacked onto the
back of the house that she had to leave when she came here. Her
first lost tooth. Something about a boy and a shed out back when
she was thirteen years old. And so I know her now, and I would
never want to take my chances on hurting the feelings of a person like Nora.

Nora's wearing a pale pink tracksuit today with thick black
stripes running down the pant legs. We all wear track suits here
at the Village, because it just makes things easier. When Nora
finally manages to bend down next to me, her pink tracksuit isn't
at all ironic. Once she's down on the floor with me, her eyes locked
onto mine, those legs of hers are suddenly quite flexible. She grips
onto my arms and I can feel all the strength of the world in her
soft, papery hands alone. I know we'll be just fine. We are both
patient, staring at each other and waiting for our strength to build
up enough. It's hard to describe how it works. Every single time,
my eyes get watery. Nora says hers get as dry as the desert. That's
when we know, without saying anything to each other, that we
are both strong enough to try to stand. It has something to do
with that three weeks of training that they made us sit through,
taking tests from the back of the workbook and getting comfortable with the idea of staring into each other's eyes. We do that
now and I try to stare beyond the cataracts floating like a skim of
ice over Nora's eyes. I've never asked her, but I like to think that
her eyes have always been blue and faded and wise, even when
she was a little girl.

Stop it, Nora says, and her grip becomes even tighter. You
stop that right now, she says. I'm lying here thinking about how
stupid I feel. I'm thinking through exactly what could have hap-

pened to me if Nora hadn't shown up and I had remained alone and stranded on the floor of this tiny kitchenette. She sees this, of course, and she tells me to stop. And when those dark thoughts start to clear away, Nora calls me Honey-doo and pulls me into a sitting position. When she sees that I'm still okay, she pulls me up to my knees. No rush, muffin, she says, her voice soft again. My legs are wobbly and they feel as empty as air, but she holds on tight. What I've realized is that we've been trained to strengthen each other in an emotional way and not just physically. When Nora looks at me, she clears away any panicked thoughts of giving up or giving in.

There's a scummy pond at the center of the parking lot, one of those man-made doo-hickies encircled by a skinny strip of overly manicured grass. A flock of loud, angry geese gathers there most days, digging into the muck with their ugly bills. There's a story that circulates among us about a woman who drowned in that pond. Maybe this was before they started the Rescuer Program, or maybe it was simply too impossible for her partner to save her. I've heard a few different versions of the story. That she drove her car into the pond. That she went for a swim because she thought she was back on her childhood farm. Various adaptations of that dead woman's story float between us like urban legend, whittled away at by the dull yet persistent blades of our old, fading minds. No matter how it happened, we do believe that she is dead and that it happened in this pond. We often gather here, talking quietly and staring at the sunlight bouncing off the greasy smooth shine of the pond's surface. We sit on the rickety benches and laugh and gasp when those geese hiss at us.

I can guarantee you that each one of us is self-conscious about how silly all of this must sound. A bunch of old folks sitting around in an elite retirement community sending out soul beacons to each other like elderly super heroes. But this is serious. I can't describe the feeling that takes over when your equilibrium first starts to go. It's not just about the technical stuff: the workings of the inner ear and balance and the weight of the body versus gravity. It's about all of your memories and experiences and moments—the stretch of your entire life—becoming suddenly off kilter, wavering precariously over the edge of nothing but blackness. We take this rescuing business seriously now that we know that it works. We know that we can help each other delay the inevitable move into the nursing home that sits adjacent to our little cluster of condominiums, its boxy shadow lurking over simply everything.

I get sucked into staring at the horrible shine of that pond's surface so easily. What if I fell in? Is that what draws us here like dusty, fading moths—the possibility? There's a strange excitement that bubbles up in me when I think about falling in there. There's a belief, tucked deep inside, that she could save me. That even though it would be impossible, she'd figure out a way. It would be Nora. Not my dead husband or my dead father or the almost dead senile Baptist preacher that lives just down the hall. It would be Nora.

wonder woman grew up in nebraska

WONDER WOMAN RIDES shotgun. She turns the radio up and rolls the window down, barely smiling as the wind whips at her and makes her hair go crazy wild. This is one of her most favorite things of all.

Lisa leans over Wonder Woman's shoulder, her chest pressed into the back of the passenger-side front seat.

"Check my breath," she says.

She pushes her face close to Wonder Woman's and opens her mouth. She exhales. Her soft, corn-colored hair slides across Wonder Woman's cheek.

"Gross," Wonder Woman says, waving her hand lazily.

"No," Lisa insists, hovering. "Just check it."

Another exhale. Wonder Woman smells green mint, from the gum that they all chew. And something else. Something empty-smelling and pleasant that she can't identify.

"You're fine," she says, reaching through Lisa's hair and placing her palm in the middle of her forehead, giving a gentle yet solid shove.

Jill, who is driving, laughs. Lisa sinks into the darkness of the backseat and giggles. All three of them laugh, at nothing.

Wonder Woman doesn't recognize the intimacy of such moments—getting close enough to check Lisa's breath or absently combing her thin fingers through Jill's hair. When the three of them are pressed tight together on her firm childhood bed, Wonder Woman does not become sentimental. Instead, she looks for vague feelings of intimacy elsewhere, in strange places like the airport bar. She won't recognize the closeness that the three of them share until years later, long after they have lost touch. Chopping vegetables for a soup late one winter afternoon in her kitchen, it will hit her. A heavy sadness, guilt in her gut.

"I shouldn't have worn this tonight," Jill says, pulling at her tight V-neck sweater with both hands and then carefully placing them back on the wheel.

"You look fine," Lisa says.

Wonder Woman says, "You look great."

Jill rolls her eyes.

Jill hates her shoulders. Lisa hates the large mole that sits on top of her right wrist. Wonder Woman hates her fingernails and bites them constantly. She doesn't know what they would look like if she left them alone. The three of them talk about these things all the time. Wonder Woman knows that there are some things they never complain about to one another, because they hate these things too much. Jill's slight overbite, for instance. Lisa's bent pinky toe. Wonder Woman never complains to them about her skin, which has a solid, milky-peach hue. "Doll flesh," she calls her complexion, to herself only, when she is especially angry.

Wonder Woman remembers liking her skin only once, when she was in the second grade and she received her first Bible at a ceremony during church. The children's Bible had colorful cartoon illustrations. Wonder Woman took hers back to her pew and held it to her chest for a few minutes before opening it during the hymn. She flipped to an illustration of a woman in a wide field. The caption read: RUTH GATHERED GRAIN IN THE FIELD. Wonder Woman thought that Ruth was pretty and brave. Brave because she looked so alone in that big field. And then she recognized that Ruth's skin was like her own, that they shared the same muted, peachy polished look. Since that Sunday, the new children's Bible open and crisp in her lap, Wonder Woman has maintained a dull, steady faith in God.

Jill drives carefully, as if to compensate for the drive home, which will be dangerous and a blur, all three of them intoxicated to some degree and giddy with the end of another somewhat lackluster Friday night. Any one of them will drive back. It's a thirty-minute drive each way. They make the trip there and back most weekends. Their fake IDs look nothing like them, especially Wonder Woman's. But some nights they aren't even carded. They're in high school. They only dare to use the fake IDs well outside of town, at the airport bar.

They approach the airport, a concrete stretch of flashing lights and hard angles and lines set against the deep night. Wonder Woman looks out the window at everything pulsing and bright and doesn't feel like she is in Nebraska anymore. The familiar, unassuming sand hills have vanished, and she doesn't mind.

Jill pulls into the visitor parking garage and tucks the ticket stub against the windshield. They move without talking, sliding out of the car and into the night. They push through glass doors and into the constant, timeless bubble of the airport. Their walk is lethargic and slow. And then the bar is in front of them, a dark, sunken room full of shadowed wood and damp rings on the counters. When you step in, you feel separate and detached, Wonder Woman thinks in a deliberate, self-conscious manner as she steps down into the airport bar. When she's here, surrounded by the must of old leather and spilled alcohol, she feels like everything—the entire world—is supposed to make sense, like she's supposed to wait around for life-altering thoughts to sift through her mind. Wonder Woman sits on her barstool and tries to force such thoughts and reflective moments. She usually leaves with a stomachache.

The drinks are cheap and strong. Lisa is the first to begin glowing from the alcohol, her cheeks and chest flooded and flushed with splotches of deep blood-red. She becomes maternal and soft. Jill becomes louder, fascinated by her own words and ideas. Wonder Woman drinks vodka tonics and margaritas and waits for herself to change. She is often disappointed. Her friends sit on either side of her, loud and flushed, and she curls her toes up in her boots until it hurts, trying to feel a change. Sometimes Wonder Woman feels like taking notes when they are at the bar and her friends begin their simultaneous metamorphoses. She feels like making painstaking, meticulous observations in a small, lined notebook. She could try to make sense of the notes later, after a very long sleep.

In the bar bathroom, Jill says, "Look at my shoulders," pulling her sweater away from her chest. "They're so wide."

The three of them stand in a row before the dim, scarred reflection of the mirror.

"My hair is so black, it's almost blue," Wonder Woman says, squinting at herself and finally, just now, beginning to feel a sweet, slight buzz.

Lisa and Jill stare at Wonder Woman's hair as if they might stroke it. There are moments like this—Lisa and Jill eyeing her like kind, sisterly predators—when Wonder Woman wonders if they are somehow jealous. When they sit together on the floor of her bedroom, Wonder Woman tucks her legs beneath herself so that Lisa and Jill won't stare at the way her knees and thighs swell over the tops of her shiny red boots.

There is a tacit dissatisfaction with these nights at the airport bar. They've been known to cry here, in the bathroom. One of them will think of something trivial—her slight overbite or her bent pinky toe or her cartoon complexion—and she'll start to cry. That moment, the crying, becomes the event of the night, or of the last few weeks. They have known each other forever. In Nebraska.

After most nights at the airport bar, and especially after a night when one of them has been crying, they pull up as close as they can get to one of the runways, the car's bumper kissing chain-link fence. They wait for a plane to fly over. If one comes, Lisa squints and shrieks. Jill stares straight ahead with blackened eyes. As the plane lifts, Wonder Woman watches her two friends and waits for the lights to wash over them. When it happens —that agreeable, clichéd image of a plane lifting low above a small, parked car—Wonder Woman feels relieved. It's important somehow.

"I'd pay a hundred dollars for that hair," Lisa says finally, staring at Wonder Woman in the mirror.

"I wouldn't," Jill says in a loud voice, pulling lip gloss from the bottom of her purse, puckering and looking only at herself now.

When Jill cries in the airport bar bathroom, Wonder Woman pats her wide shoulders and brushes back her hair, secretly feeling vindicated and pleased.

"Bingo," Jill says for no particular reason, smacking her glossy lips and smiling at herself in the mirror. Her eyes get wide, like she's about to pounce on something just behind the mirror and squeeze it ecstatically. Squeeze it until it's good and dead and gone.

A couple of years before, when Wonder Woman was baby-sitting one night, Jill called and convinced her to come meet her and Lisa at Jill's house, which was a few streets over. Wonder Woman was about to put the baby down for the night.

"There's no way I can leave him here alone," she told Jill.

"Just for a little bit," Jill snapped back. "He'll be asleep. He'll be fine."

Wonder Woman was in a daze when she placed the sleeping five-month-old in his crib, baby formula drying on his wrinkled lips. She locked the front door and walked over to Jill's house, picturing what could happen to the baby. He could suffocate. He could choke on something. He could be engulfed in a fire. He could wake up and cry out and no one would come. Jill and Lisa acted aloof when she showed up that night, as if she had decided to drop by without being invited. Wonder Woman stayed for an excruciating hour, perched on the edge of Jill's bed, watching the two of them read magazines. When she said, "I'm going," Jill looked over at Lisa and raised her eyebrows, not saying a word. When she got back, Wonder Woman stared at the sleeping baby for a full ten minutes, fighting several waves of nausea.

Nothing like that has happened since then. But Wonder Woman still thinks about what dangerous thing Jill might demand next. She wishes she knew what it was, that she could just get it over with.

There's a man sitting on Wonder Woman's barstool when they return from their first trip of the night to the bathroom. The three of them slow down and stare. This has never happened before. They'd staked their claim; there's a jacket or a sweater draped over each one of their stools. They stop and stand there for a moment. Wonder Woman waits for one of them to think of something to say. She stares at the man's back. Most weekends they come here, to the airport bar, and get drunk and stay bored. But now there's a man perched on Wonder Woman's stool, the backs of his thighs pressed into her favorite sweater. Her most favorite of all. And it feels like they've gotten lucky tonight. Wonder Woman stares at the small patch of woolly hair peeking just above the man's shirt collar and feels like a big plane is flying especially low, just above their car. Lights shining and sweeping. The windows rolled all the way down.

One day during lunch at school, Lisa and Jill had dared Wonder Woman to throw her taco condiments onto Ms. Pearson, their math teacher. The three of them often sit alone at lunch, in a tight row along one side of the cafeteria table, as if they are lined up in the dim airport bar. They watch the other students and come up with dares. They never go through with them. But this one afternoon, Wonder Woman did. She felt bold and buoyant, so different from when she had abandoned the baby. She took the tiny plastic cup of cheese and the tiny plastic cup of pasty guacamole and threw. Ms. Pearson was facing away from them. The two cups bounced off her back, leaving a little green trail on the left shoulder of her brown blazer. Lisa slapped the cafeteria table with both hands and Jill closed her eyes. Wonder Woman stood up before Ms. Pearson turned around. "I tripped," she said, and Ms. Pearson nodded blandly. She'd never suspect Wonder Woman of anything.

Wonder Woman now sees herself the way she thinks her friends sometimes see her since the incident in the cafeteria—a bit taller, holding the possibility of surprising things somewhere within her. They didn't ignore her after that, like they had during the babysitting incident. Every once in a while, she feels that Lisa and Jill are quietly waiting for her to do something again, to let herself go and let them watch. She feels that now, standing beside them and staring at the strange man whose buttocks are pressed firmly into her favorite sweater.

"Excuse me," she says, walking up to the bar. "That's my sweater." She nods at the stool and feels heat swirling in the palms of her hands. The man's eyes are blue. For some reason, she imagines a heavy, golden light surrounding him, a halo of surprise and possibility here in the airport bar.

"Well," he says, standing.

He grabs his drink and walks to an empty table at the back of the bar, near the bathroom.

The three of them sit on their stools. They order more drinks. They act as if small things like this happen all the time at the airport bar. But Wonder Woman knows that each one of them is secretly pleased and excited. Unpredictable moments are rare. Now they have one they can remember and reclaim over and over again. Wonder Woman drinks and feels a ticklish spark within her, like the gentle, steady blip of a radar. She had felt this same prickly buzzing when she took the taco condiments into her hands and threw without thinking.

"Do you think he's watching us?" Jill whispers.

"Gross," Lisa says, twisting her head over her shoulder and looking toward the back of the bar.

"You think it's creepy?" Wonder Woman asks her.

Lisa shrugs and then finishes her drink. "Anyway," she says, "he's not even looking at us."

"Who cares," says Jill.

The rest of the night is an uneventful blur of nothing much to say. Neither Lisa nor Jill comment on Wonder Woman's bold move. The three of them stare at one another and at their hands. They raise their drinks to their lips. Wonder Woman tries to feel the tiny blip of radar, which has faded into nothing at all.

"Quit jiggling your foot," Jill hisses at Wonder Woman. Lisa looks down at her hands, and Wonder Woman hooks both feet in the barstool so that they are tight and motionless.

They avoid the bathroom until the man leaves his table and walks out of the bar a couple of hours later. Wonder Woman watches him go, forcing that imaginary golden light to leave with him. She can almost see it sliding along behind him if she squints just right. Then the three of them rush to the back of the bar, flushed and squabbling over who gets to go first, dizzy from the anticipated relief.

Later that night, on the way to their car, they see him in the parking garage. He is bent over on the concrete, kneeling in an empty parking space with his head in his hands. Wonder Woman is the first to see him, and she doesn't say anything to Lisa or Jill. She sees that his nose is bleeding. Because he has been drinking, it probably won't stop anytime soon. This is something she thinks she learned in a middle school health class. She stares at his shoulders. They hardly move when he breathes.

Lisa sees him next, and she squeals quietly. She sounds like a child on her birthday or on Christmas morning, but her face is splotchy and twisted. They stop walking and stare. The man is still several yards away. This is the oddest thing that they've seen in the airport parking garage so far. One time they saw a man step out of his car and then pull a Magic Eight ball out of the passenger seat. He had looked certain of something after tipping it and reading the message. Then he showed up alone at the airport bar later that night, looking around. By the time Wonder Woman and her friends left he was still alone, looking disappointed, but not surprised.

Wonder Woman can feel the buzzing sensation start up within her as they stand and watch the bleeding man. She doesn't think he has seen them yet, even after Lisa's little squeal. Again, Wonder Woman has a guilty, delicious pit in her stomach—this is a moment they will remember. Because of this moment, from now on there will be a twinge of possibility in the car each night that they drive to the airport bar. Something to keep them coming back again and again.

Wonder Woman walks over to the man and kneels beside him. She feels shiny and warm. She feels like crying. She feels like flying, like diving into the ocean from miles above the waves. Then she sees him up close. He is grotesque and pale. There's a slight metallic smell. His hands are too big for his face. This could have happened to the baby when I left him alone that night, Wonder Woman thinks. Somehow, this is exactly the disaster she had tried to imagine while sitting on the edge of Jill's bed: blood and spit and pavement. But she's not afraid now. She senses her friends watching her in disbelief, horror tinged with awkward jealousy, and she doesn't care what they think.

When the man looks up at her, thin blood running along the sides of his mouth and dripping from his chin, Wonder Woman doesn't flinch. She feels shouldered with a heavy, insistent burden. This is not the tired, familiar sensation that all people her age feel—the dramatic burden of adolescence. This particular sensation is different, a feeling that Lisa and Jill will never experience. But Wonder Woman doesn't know this yet, like so many other things. She thinks everything is the same. She looks at the man's face, not understanding that the childlike urge she sometimes has to change the world is not simply teenage angst. She just feels the radar blipping like mad, her limbs shaking. The golden light seems real now, thick and textured. She can barely turn her head through it.

Lisa and Jill stay far away from the bleeding man. Wonder Woman thinks she can hear Lisa crying. Then the man says something that Wonder Woman can't understand. She looks closely at his face, and he mumbles it again: "I'm no one. Don't worry." She notices the deep pores on his face, the dry lines working their way out from behind his ears and into the corners of his eyes. He breathes. She realizes her arms are gently looped around his neck. She hadn't known that she had touched him. She feels drunk, extremely drunk, for the first time. She feels heavy and sad and relieved. He's squatting there, and she's touching him. He says it once again, his voice thick with self-pity and booze: "I'm no one." Wonder Woman senses the drama and weariness in what he says. She recognizes the stale banality of such a scene: a drunken man, alone, with blood on his face. He is a lesson. He has been set here for these young girls to see, a clear example of loneliness and danger and ordinary pain. Wonder Woman knows that what he has said is true, that she has brought this truth out of him, and she is not frightened. There is no forced ache in her stomach from trying to think and believe in something profound and meaningful. These thoughts simply fly through her and touch her as she inhales and exhales. It doesn't hurt one bit. Apparently that glow—the yellowish, golden light—is perfectly one hundred percent real.

Wonder Woman drives home that night. Both Lisa and Jill sit in the back. There's a ghostly empty space in the passenger seat. Wonder Woman wants to reach into it, but she keeps both hands on the wheel. The man had insisted that she leave him alone after she helped him into his car. He had sat slumped at the wheel and waved them on, trying to grin. Blood in his teeth. Wonder Woman doesn't pull up to one of the runways and wait for a plane. There are no protests from the backseat. Lisa and Jill are blank canvases now. They have empty eyes. All of that change has once again been wiped straightaway. Wonder Woman will remain curious for a very long time yet, wanting to take jealous notes on the ways in which her two friends transform into cleaner, tighter versions of themselves while at the airport bar.

They dodge fate once again that night. There is no car accident, no smashed windows or heads. Years later, Wonder Woman will compare the stupid, lucky magic of how they always somehow managed to get home safe from the airport bar to other, scarier things. But at this particular moment, she simply drives them into the dark, dark night, unaware for now of what it is that they all, each one of them, are driving from.

edith and the ocean dome

> I was the best harvester. Tell them that. Tell them I
> made more money than my husband. Tell them that.
> —*from an interview with an ama diver,*
> *Jolie Bookspan's "The Mermaid Stories"*

THE HEAT IS like a cupped hand, and Edith is a tiny pearl trapped right at the center of it. She is a fish, she decides. The air is that wet and that thick. Edith stands still with her arms pressed into her sides. If she moves them at all she will brush against another body, someone chattering and smiling and oblivious to her. When a grumble starts to shake the base of the huge, fake volcano and then fire is suddenly spewing from its mouth, someone near Edith says, "Is this really happening?" The wave machine turns on at the same time, and Edith is transfixed by the plastic sheen of each magnificently perfect wave. Is this really happening? She sings this to herself in her head. She lets the question roll around loosely and she admires it from a lazy distance. The heat is too heavy and too wet for active thought. There are too many people pressed in close to her—screaming children and shrugging adults, bodies throwing themselves into the sudden, turquoise waves. Is this really happening? She has no idea if the person who asked this question had a foreign accent. They could have been American or something else entirely. With what seems like an awkward mix of heavy metal and classical music pumping through the speakers, along with the white noise of millions of gallons of rushing water, it's impossible to tell. And so for once in her life, Edith—standing there in the fake sand in her pitiful sun dress, her best one—doesn't try to decipher a single thing.

If Edith closes her eyes, this is it, the entirety of her life. All of these strange voices fuse together into one perfect pitch of not having a care in the world. The chlorine stings her nostrils. The heat pushes into every part of her. Everything that Edith knows about the sea, the years of careful and meticulous research, disappears. Edith is in Japan. She is on the beautiful, rocky island of Kyushu. But when she looks up, the sky is painted on, an empty cerulean blue with static, pure white clouds. All of this is contained in the Ocean Dome and Edith has no idea, really, what's outside the water park. She pushes her toes into the soft, cool sand that has been engineered to not stick to her skin and feels like there is no need to know.

Most of the people pressed near her on the fake beach are in their bathing suits. Edith thinks about going back to the hotel and changing into her swimsuit. She hasn't unpacked yet. The flight was long. She needs a nap. But she can't move away from the rolling surf. The humidity of the indoor water park, something about the artificiality of it all, pressure cooks Edith's insides. A sense of self-consciousness that feels oddly soothing begins to bubble to the surface. Edith is reflective, something she is most definitely not used to. She stares at a group of college-aged men wading out into the cookie cutter waves and thinks: Wow, I've been with a lot of men in my life. Followed by: Wow. I refuse to settle down. Edith is transfixed. She finds herself lining up all of her ex-lovers and ex-boyfriends in her mind. She is certain that each one of them would love this place, the world's largest indoor pool. The conditions that are always perfect for surfing. The rows of restaurants with balconies overlooking the fake surf below. The artificial palm trees swaying in the artificial breeze, and the horrible music. Edith has never brought a boyfriend along on a research trip. She consciously chooses men who get a bored, lost look when she talks about her work. This helps her maintain a clear distinction between her work life and her personal life, which doesn't really exist. Her home base is Cleveland, the place where she grew up. During her brief breaks between research trips, she will often call a man she has been seeing off and on and set up a date for an unmemorable movie followed by strong drinks and maybe after that dutiful sex. She might bring him back to her studio apartment. The place is so tiny that she often wakes up with the sensation of being stuffed into the tight cabin of a ship. But when she is home in Cleveland, she gets sick without the constant rocking of waves. And if a man is there sleeping beside her, she gets sick without the solitude.

Edith feels a bit delirious and lightheaded and yet eerily calm. She can almost see the crowd of her exes pushing through the mass of people on the beach and diving into the waves. Suddenly, that's all she can think about. Not her research. And not this strange emptiness resting here on her back and shoulders that she has flown straight across the world to ponder.

EDITH had decided on this trip while standing in the pathetic seafood section in the grocery store down the street from her place in Cleveland. She was between research trips and sucked into the funk that she often falls into while at home, wading through logs

and graphs of data and doing a bit of freelance work while waiting for the next trip out to sea. Edith had just spent five months
living on an atoll in the middle of the Indian Ocean, thousands
of miles from civilization. Atolls—sets of tiny coral islands strung
together like ribbon, ringing a pristine lagoon in the middle of
the open sea—are Edith's main area of research. On this particular trip, she had spent hundreds of hours scuba diving in the lagoon, studying sea turtles and spinner dolphins and finger coral
and green bubble algae. Then she was back home in the grayness
of Cleveland, gearing herself up to call someone for a sub-par
date, staring at the rows of limp, orange salmon on display in the
grocery store. The plastic bristle of the graying shrimp. The lethargic lobsters in their tiny holding tank, their claws held tight
with rubber bands. Suddenly, Edith felt paralyzed. It was then,
during that horrible paralysis, that she decided on this trip. And
as she decided, Edith understood that it had been sitting in the
back of her mind for a very long time—this idea of flying across
the world in order to pursue family lore, something personal
rather than scientific. This frightened her tremendously.

She booked her flight and her hotel room that same night.
Sitting in her dark apartment with only the glow of her laptop,
she saw the flashing, glitzy ad for the Ocean Dome and clicked
on it and entered her credit card information before she could
think. Something about the outrageous nature of the water park
seemed soothing to Edith. When she traveled, she slept in tiny
bunks on boats or in one-room shacks with thatched roofs. She
needed to stay somewhere like the Ocean Dome, she decided, so
that she could classify this trip as something new. Something personal rather than work-related. Edith wanted to call her mother.
She wanted to call her aunts, too. She wanted to tell them that
she was going to look into all those stories of a mysterious Japanese ancestor she had grown up listening to them spout off. She

wanted to invite them, insist that this needed to be a girls' geta-
way. But Edith did none of those things, and now here she was all
by herself at this ridiculously huge resort trying to figure out exactly what to do.

THE first few days of the trip all feel exactly the same. Edith
finds herself shifting endlessly between her hotel room, the water park, and the hotel bar, a dark, sunken room with a massive
aquarium set in the middle of the liquor shelves. She slips into
her swimsuit, a modest one piece with wide shoulder straps, before going to the water park. But she has yet to get into the water.
There are no fish. There are no mollusks or whales or floating
plankton. If she gets into that water, there is no threat of something mysterious brushing against her shins, no potential sting
or bite. And for some reason, that empty sense of safety un-
nerves Edith.

The giant roof of the Ocean Dome is retractable, and on most
days it is open. Edith sits in the fake sand and sunbathes. This is
the first time that she can remember allowing herself such an aim-
less luxury. She loves the tight seal of the park and how walled
off from the rest of the world she feels. She can stretch out on her
back and let her mind float. Here in the park, she is not moored
down by data and the logistics of various measurements and ex-
periments. There is nothing to study in the park, nothing to quan-
tify or classify. The fake palm fronds do not photosynthesize.
The chlorine kills off anything that might try to grow in the water. Sure, maybe she would discover traces of red slime bacteria,
which is common in indoor pools, if she really looked. But she's
not going to. Edith had never realized how endless her work is.
The things that she studies in the sea are constantly blooming
and hatching and blossoming, opening up into even more. Here
Edith lolls beneath the hot sun on the cool sand and does not

think of those things. When the retractable roof is closed, during a stray afternoon shower or in the early evening, Edith sunbathes beneath the painted sky, her pale skin still slathered in SPF 50.

By the fifth day, Edith is no longer dizzy from how often the employees of the resort bow to her. When she asks for directions to the spa, when she orders her breakfast, when she nods hello and smiles, the men and women bow as if it is as natural as blinking, bobbing right back up and going about their affairs. It all seems synchronized. But then she starts to notice that one particular bellhop's bow is a little looser, his eyes always smiling. Edith walks past him, through the open airiness of the hotel's luxurious lobby, and he bows each time, watching her. Immediately, Edith is wary. Her elbows and knees lock up. She feels excited and squirrelly and a little nauseous all at once. This again. It is always one single, simple thing that strikes Edith and makes her think a man might be right for her. One single thing that sucks her in and makes her believe in an instant. A blushing jaw line. A slight stutter. Shaggy sideburns. An old, rusted bicycle. And now it is this man with the lazy bow, trying to make her feel as if he watches her in a way that is different from how he glances at any other woman or man crossing from one end of the huge, expansive lobby to the next. Edith finds herself scoping him out each time she enters the lobby. As usual, her sudden interest in the man feels synthetic, like an imitation of someone else's life. It is as if she has pulled on an old, familiar Halloween mask; she can smell the musty, tart scent of her breath still leftover from the last time she wore it.

Edith knows that the water park is ridiculous. She knows that she needs to get out onto the island and explore, focus on why she came here in the first place. According to Edith's mother and aunts, they have an ancestor from this rocky island. Edith is determined to track down the origin of that story, no matter how impossible the task, and pin it as true or untrue. But each time she finds herself standing at the magnificent corner window in her hotel room—the Pacific an open mouth to the west, the city's mirrored skyscrapers winking at her from the east, the mountains beyond—she can't manage to squint out the huge, white oval of the Ocean Dome twenty-four stories below her. She's been sucked into a netherworld. The Italian restaurant sits right at the top of the volcano, and this is where Edith has a glass of wine each evening right around sunset, when they close the retractable roof and run a laser light show against the phony, walled horizon. I am a tourist, Edith thinks to herself, testing out the concept. This is a vacation, she decides. The sunset laser light show lasts a solid twelve minutes each evening, the wave machine running full blast with pinks and reds and purples dancing in the water.

In her mind, Edith does practice how she might begin to ask around about the ama. *Women divers?* she might say, flapping her arms at her sides like a fish. *The ama divers? In the sea?* with a gesture out toward where she thinks the coastline might be. She's indoors all the time, either in the hotel or in the water park, and so it's easy to forget the geography that surrounds her on the island. This is a strange, new sensation for Edith—not always knowing exactly where the sea is. The disorientation makes her feel drugged and airy. Even when she is living on an atoll and working in the lagoon with her back constantly to the ocean, she can feel it there pushing up against her. At the resort, she forgets the real ocean entirely for hours at a time.

Most of the resort employees speak only a little broken English. Edith smiles and waves at the women behind the front desk each time she passes through the lobby and imagines trying to explain to them what she has come out here to find. *Ama divers,* she might say. *I think I'm related. Ancestor.* She orders an amaretto sour and eyes the bartender, trying to work up the courage. *Women of the sea. Abalone. Where are the ama?* And each time she envisions such a conversation, her arms are flapping at her sides like a screwy fish, as if this will somehow dissolve the language barrier and make things clear. How does she break her story up into easily understandable bits? *Family legend,* she might say. *My mothers and her sisters. A crazy idea. The women divers here at Kyushu. There's a story. That I'm family. They are family.* Her arms flapping. *Do they exist?*

Edith walks through the lobby and watches the bellhop with the funny bow watch her. He's the one she should ask about the ama. Before this trip, she made a pitiful list of Japanese words that might be helpful. She could spout these words off to the bellhop, if only she knew how to pronounce them. *Awabi. Nawa. Fudoshi. Iso nageki. Tengugui. Tegane. Oke. Namako.* Edith sees the bellhop and thinks about asking him about the ama, but then he bows to her and she gets all locked up. Any idea of doing research out on the island disappears.

THE Ocean Dome's roof is open and sunlight shoots into the park like a laser beam, ferocious and intense. Edith lounges on the sand and props herself on her elbows to watch a group of Australian surfers with longish, sun-bleached hair. They chat and laugh between waves, but then they are serious once they are up on their boards. When the wave machine shuts off, the surfers start cliff diving from one of the foam rock ledges midway up the volcano. Edith is sure that it's not allowed, but no one stops them. The men are good looking and easy going. Edith crosses her ankles, again thinking about the men she has dated. She can see them all together here in a pack. They transform from pasty, nondescript thirty-something and forty-something-year-olds with the whisper of a possible receding hairline into vigorous men. Here in the park, away from Cleveland, they are shirtless and chiseled and they pat each other on their broad, tanned backs a lot. If they were here together they would surf for hours, each of them shooting by Edith on the treadmill of immaculate waves. Edith is a bit surprised that she never realized how much her exes would get along and how few of them actually know each other. She could have them shipped out here for a strange kind of reunion. An adventure. Edith has no idea what the nightlife in this city is like, but her pack of reinvented men would sniff it out in an instant. No longer boring and aging and sluggishly awkward, they would roar and dance. And Edith would be there, somewhere at their sides, while they had the time of their lives.

A shadow falls over Edith's legs. When she looks up, the bellhop with the lazy bow is crouching above her, his hands on his knees. He looks down at her and she feels like a sea squirt he's just discovered in a tide pool.

"Hello?" Edith says.

And he says, "Hello?"

She nods and smiles. He bows his head, watching her.

"You burn out here," he says, pointing at her shins.

"Oh," Edith says. "Sunblock." She nods toward the giant tube resting on her beach bag.

"You burn," he says, smiling.

"I'm careful," Edith says.

He keeps smiling, and Edith has no idea if he understands what she has just said.

"I'm careful," she says again, shrugging her shoulders cheerily, as if she can shrug the UV rays right off her skin.

"You burn," he says again, nodding, bowing, and then turning to walk away.

Sweat pours off of Edith's upper lip as she watches the bellhop leave. She refuses to admit how excited this strange interaction has made her, and so she blames the profuse sweating on the intense heat. She even considers finally getting into the water and pulling herself beneath the surface for some relief from the sun. But she just can't do it. Something shifts and stutters in her chest. Not fear, exactly. But the emptiness of the little body of water does seem threatening in a way. Edith has banged on the nose of an aggressive bull shark with her fist. She has unwound a gruesome, fiery bangle of jellyfish tentacles from her ankle. Using a tiny fishing knife, she sawed off the head of a seven foot moray eel that bit her hand and refused to let go, even after she dragged it up onto the diving boat. These things did not scare Edith. When it comes to the ocean, what scares Edith are the deepest trenches. The darkest reaches. And for some reason, the clear blue water in this contained, man-made park makes Edith think of those places and the few creatures that manage to survive there. Tiny shrimp that secrete clouds of luminescence and then scurry away. Minnow-sized fish with fragile skeletons and enormous mouths and sharp teeth, able to swallow things ten times bigger than themselves. These deep-sea creatures lurk in the shadows of Edith's imagination. And, oddly enough, Edith can envision them beneath the surface of the harmless looking wave pool.

A few days later the bellhop crouches over Edith's beach towel yet again. He shakes his head softly at her and then glances up at the opening in the retractable roof, as if he could order it to close with his mind if he wanted to, in order to protect her.

"I'm careful," Edith says again.

It's the only thing she can think to say as she scans the smooth planes of his face.

"Water feels good," he says, nodding toward the waves lapping near her feet.

Edith remembers that she does not know this person who is crouched above her. It's so easy to feel naked with only her swimsuit on.

"I'm sure it does," she says.

He smiles in a slow, kind way. Has he opened her up like a locked drawer? Did he need only one quick glance in order to understand her strange, irrational fear? Something lets loose in

Edith's chest. She is turned off. Just like that. She tries to smile up at the bellhop and at the sun without grimacing. This scares Edith sometimes: how fast her impressions of people, especially men, can change. Most of her relationships have been a sickening, constant back and forth affair full of mixed emotions and indecisiveness, like an old state fair ride. At the beginning, she has to force herself to get on and strap herself in, huge, desperate laughs rolling up from somewhere deep inside of her.

Edith watches the bellhop walk away again. He has his bellhop uniform on, of course, and he looks so out of place as he tries to negotiate the sand in his hard-soled work shoes. The thick polyester of his burgundy suit must be suffocating. But Edith can tell, even from watching the back of his head, that he's smiling as he nods at the people he has to weave through on the beach. She watches his body in freeze frame, peeling away layers with each step, every part of him carefully scrutinized and cataloged. It has always been this way for Edith. She can't help but turn men into specimens, dissecting them away into nothing but a pile of parts and pieces, delicate cross sections of bone and gristle and mysterious urges. The young engineer with the hairless arms who worked for her mother. The guy at the post office with the bum knee. The butcher with the short, stunted tongue.

Emotional klutz. The phrase pushes up behind Edith's eye sockets as she shifts around on top of her beach towel. She can't find a comfortable position. The delicious feeling of being on vacation has evaporated. She feels as useless as a beached whale. And hopeless. That, too, of course.

FOR the past ten years, Edith has been waiting for her mother to ask her about when she might settle down, meet someone nice and have a couple kids. Edith has been waiting for the opportunity to explain to her mother how the female octopus rejects the male after they mate. She alone shields and protects the eggs for over a month. She oxygenates them with squirts of water. She vacuum cleans them with her suction cups. So intent on her duties, she stops eating and begins to starve. She dies shortly after the birth of her offspring, amid the swarm of 200,000 progeny. Most of them are eaten right away. One, maybe two, lives to reproduce. Edith waits for her mother to corner her with this question of a husband and family, maybe during a late night call while Edith is somewhere on shore during a research trip, or maybe during a rare, fancy brunch in Cleveland. But her mother does not mention it. She is happy, it seems, with her daughter's strange, solitary life. Why does this unnerve Edith? Why does she want to lash out at her sweet, supportive mother with the story of the female octopus and shameless sacrifice? Edith's mother is in her late sixties and is fit and happy and kind. She would be the perfect grandmother. Edith is her only child. Her mother watches the lives of her numerous nieces and nephews with nothing like envy, and Edith is baffled.

ON the eighth morning, Edith wakes up with a hard shell of heat radiating across her entire body. She lies still for a few moments, thinking she is dreaming of the sun, thinking she is on the fake beach and she has fallen asleep on her towel. When she opens her eyes and stretches her arms above her head, the skin on her chest and arms screams. She curls her toes and the tops of her shins burn and buzz.

"I've been burnt," Edith says out loud, to the empty hotel room.

She's still half asleep, still trying to make sense of where she is. The hotel bed is a cool, soft, downy cloud against her hot body. For a moment, the irrational subconscious part of Edith's brain that is already retreating convinces her that something horribly devious has occurred. Someone sneaked into her room in the middle of the night and held a blow torch against her skin. Someone rubbed fire coral along her entire body. Someone lassoed the sun and pulled it in here, anchoring it just above her bed.

"Oh," Edith says, wincing as she sits up.

She presses her palms, the only cool part of her body, against her hot skin, trying to soothe random patches. The skin on her chest and arms is itchy, scattered with angry, red pimples.

Edith shivers during the elevator ride down to the lobby. She feels intoxicated. She feels as if she has cracked the valve on her scuba tank and then rode it, shooting to the surface like a giant squid. She sees her bellhop at his spot next to the middle revolving door. As she walks toward him through the cold hotel air, her head pulses and aches. He begins to bow when he sees her but then stops. She likes this, his hesitation and obvious concern. Even as her head throbs and screams, Edith thinks, *Take that as a sign.* And she is so feverish and chilled that she wonders if she might have said it out loud. She is wrapped up in her huge hotel robe, a fluffy white marshmallow with an angry red center, her chest a burning coal. She gets the usual bows from the other employees in the lobby. They watch her with no apparent shock, as if they have seen this many times before.

"No more showers," the bellhop says as soon as Edith has reached him.

"My skin," Edith says, holding out her white cushioned arms like a zombie.

"Only baths," he says. "For your skin."

Edith lurches over to one of the sitting areas that is enveloped in a forest of massive potted ferns. She winces as her body hits the cushioned chair. The bellhop is at her side in moments with a silver tray holding a tea set.

"Green tea," he says. "Drink slowly. Drink a lot."

He hands her a small jar of something that looks gelatinous and strange. Edith wonders if it is an ancient remedy, some family secret that he is handing over to her like it's nothing. She unscrews the lid and smells the familiar, empty-melon scent.

"Aloe," she says. "Of course."

"Allergy," he says, nodding toward the bit of red skin on her chest that is exposed.

"I'm allergic to the sun?"

"You are sweating," he says.

"I'm hot and cold."

Edith is fair-skinned and she has always been careful while working on the sea, keeping herself slathered in sunblock and sitting beneath awnings on research boats, wearing T-shirts while skin diving. This is the first time she's ever had sun poisoning. After all of these years, this is her skin's rebellion. Something about the tight seal of the Ocean Dome had made Edith feel reckless. She had worn sunblock, yes, but she had also stretched herself out beneath the opening in that roof for hours, her body prone to the sun like any other mindless tourist.

"You need rest," the bellhop says.

He has sat down in the chair next to hers, and Edith realizes that they are being watched by the women behind the front desk. A new wave of chills crashes down over Edith's shoulders and runs the length of her spine. It feels good in such a strange way. Edith's skin is hot and itchy and swollen, but she feels refreshed, too. She feels like an egg that is about to hatch at any moment. A ripe, furry melon ready to be sliced neatly in two. The knife would sink in so easily, with just the slightest pressure.

"I'm Edith," she says.

And he says, "I'm Jun."

"That's so nice," she says, staring at the glossy dimple on each of his knuckles.

"I'm here because of a rumor," Edith says. "I guess that's what you would call it," she says. "A family rumor."

The cool air on her skin pushes the story out of her in one smooth movement. Edith tells Jun how her mother and her aunts have always mentioned a Japanese ancestor from this island, a woman who held her breath and dove deep into the sea for seaweed and shellfish.

"It's all perfectly ridiculous," Edith says. "I don't even know where the story came from. How anyone would have ever heard of this island. The women in my family talk about it like it makes perfect sense."

The stories are saturated with stereotype, and Edith is too feverish in this moment to be self-conscious of that as she tells Jun about them. She remembers her mother and her aunts flitting about the kitchen when she was a kid, before something big like Thanksgiving or a birthday celebration. The ama story would come up and these women would claim the smooth skin, the thick hair, the quiet fortitude from this shadowy ancestor. They would claim things that none of them really had.

"So I've been looking into it," Edith says. "I've been doing some research in general."

Compared to her professional work, Edith's research for this trip had been pathetic. She spent a couple hours on Google and Wikipedia and then booked a flight on-line that same evening.

Jun has been nodding the entire time. Edith knows he hasn't understood everything she has just said, but she doesn't care. She decides not to tell him about her work as a scientist. To him, she just wants to be the lost tourist with a strange story.

"These women," Edith says. "I want to go see them. But I don't."

She laughs at her own confusion.

"Ama-san," Jun says. "I can take you."

He looks at her as if he can see the entire story, her secret ob-session since she was a little girl, stiff-spined and balled up inside of her chest like a sea urchin.

After days of putting this off, everything feels too easy.

"You decide," Jun says. "But first you rest."

Edith stares at his knuckles and his long fingers and she nods. The itching on her skin feels like a mimeograph of how she could feel for this man. The racking and the buzzing all over her body feels oddly familiar. It's difficult, in her delirious state, to separate the sun poisoning from any possible attraction she might feel to-ward Jun, a stranger. Edith's physical sensations when she is around men are often robotic and alien. Pulsing thighs and beat-ing palms that feel entirely separate from her. These sensations are more interesting to her than the sex itself.

Edith pulls herself back into the cool pocket of her bed and spends the rest of the day there. She slathers her skin in aloe. The air touches her like a cold, cold whisper as solid as ice.

EDITH is feverish for two more days after that. She spends much of the time in the hotel bar, alternating between seltzer with vodka and seltzer without. She squints at the fish in the massive aquar-ium until they become blurry blotches of darting color, cartoon-ish and unclassifiable. Edith finds herself constantly envisioning the group of her exes here at the resort. Perhaps these near-hallucinations are a product of the fevered pulsing beneath her skin infused with the alcohol. This place, with its fake ecosystem and the real ocean just beyond, seems to be a breeding ground for strange thoughts. Edith can see these men so vividly lined up at the bar, squinting at the fish right along with her. They are always shirtless, always smiling and patting each other on the back. Not paying too much attention to her, exactly, but making things cheery and pleasant and all around nice. Maybe sometimes they elbow each other, their eyebrows inappropriately raised in unison at the solid, stiff bows of the resort employees. Edith is often drawn to men who are too immature for their age, men who ignore the poof of sudden bellies and the sagging of chins, men who refuse to commit to anything. She herself has always been too old and too serious for her age. Maybe it's the curse of a name like Edith. She has scrutinized photos of herself as a newborn: the lips tightly pursed, the eyes piercing and even condescending. Nothing, her mother often tells her in her cheery voice, has ever been good enough for Edith.

Edith can't stay away from the water park. She dresses in cotton pants and long-sleeved shirts and then wraps the big white hotel robe around herself like a cloak. The humid heat outside the hotel makes her skin throb. In the park, Edith huddles beneath the pizzeria's awning, near the lazy river that is clogged with inner-tubes, and watches the surfers when the spewing volcano signals a new hour and the wave machine is turned on. She wears an expensive, wide-brimmed hat from the hotel gift shop and a huge pair of sunglasses. She feels like an exotic, ritzy leper. The pizzeria does not serve vodka tonics. Edith drinks several Diet Cokes until she thinks she can feel the acidic carbonation thrumming through every part of her. The noises of the park fall into one flat wash and Edith tries to pull herself back into memories of her childhood. She flips through them like the pages of a children's book that have become so familiar they are now strange. It's impossible to focus, to make sense of anything.

Her mother and aunts back in Cleveland are used to never quite knowing where Edith has gone off to this time. They patiently wait for sun-worn postcards, salted and wilted from the sea, and tack them proudly throughout their kitchens. But there is a reason why Edith did not tell her mother or her aunts about this particular trip. There is a reason why she has never asked them for more information about the ama story. As a kid, Edith was outside of that tight group of women. And even now, as an adult, she is still on the periphery. This isn't simply because they are family women and Edith is not. This isn't simply because they have forever been so strong and obvious in their carpools and red sauces and monogamy. It is because Edith is a different animal altogether and she always has been. Something didn't quite fuse together when she was washing around in her mother's womb, waiting for the genetic makeup of a long history of settled, content, mid-western women to burrow down into her core. Or perhaps something wound around something else too tightly. Regardless, Edith is not made like the other women in her family. And now, out here on this island, swallowed up within her thick robe and the thick heat of the water park, Edith likes to think that she can feel the blood of the mysterious ama ancestor pumping through her, suddenly activated because she came out here. She can feel that blood shooting through her arteries and veins like a poison-tipped arrow, making her itch and burn and suddenly understand, well, something.

JUN leaves hot pots of green tea outside Edith's door several times a day. She drinks it nonstop and begins to feel better, like she's falling back into her own skin bit by bit. When Edith lived in an underwater lab that was tethered to the floor of a deep atoll lagoon, she was amazed by how quickly her skin healed from scrapes and cuts, even those embedded with bits of rough coral. Up here on dry land, she heals slowly. While the horrible rash begins to clear from Edith's skin, the itching and stinging still flares up unexpectedly.

Jun leaves notes with the green tea, tucked under the tiny cups and saucers.

My grandfather say ama dive through pregnancy. My grand-father say ama wear infants on their back when they dive.

Ama tie rope around her waist and dive down. Husband or brother sit in boat. Comfortable, singing songs. Waiting.

Diving begins here in Kyushu. First of all villages.

People believe ama are ghosts.

Ama whistle when she breathes. Sad song before dive.

Jun's handwriting is clear and careful, and Edith can hear his voice when she reads the notes. Compared to the stiff articles she writes for various science journals, Jun's writing is poetry. Sometimes Edith does freelance work for tourist magazines and she has so much trouble trying to pierce through the formality of her work into something that feels fun and carefree and enticing and human.

Edith already knows about the ama from her research online. She knows about the men waiting on the surface in boats and she knows about the long whistling sound a woman makes before she pulls herself beneath the surface. She's not sure about infants riding the backs of their mothers. She does not believe in ghosts. But she loves how Jun hands her these ideas as if they are more than facts, as if they are relics of a history he is actually connected to. Edith envies the freedom of simply telling a story, no fact checking, no exact measurements or controls.

Edith comes back to her room from the bar one evening and finds a brochure tucked beneath yet another hot pot of tea. On the front there is a dated, grainy photograph of two Japanese women smiling hugely, topless with white cloth tied over their hair. Each holds a large shellfish in her hands. Edith takes the brochure over to her bed and crawls to the middle of the mattress before unfolding it and reading. She knows these things already. That the ama are a dying breed. That most women divers on islands like Kyushu are over fifty years old with no successors. That the ama have been diving for shellfish and seaweed for at least two thousand years. They burn salt during purifying rituals before their dives. They can endure cold temperatures for awe inspiring amounts of time. Their bodies build up and withstand unbelievable amounts of carbon dioxide, baffling scientists for decades. In ancient times, the abalone collected by the ama was used as tax payments. It was dried and cut into long strips by priests, served to the samurai for vigor, fastened to congratulatory gift envelopes. The ama use a sharp, spatula-shaped tool to cut the meaty, dome-shelled abalone away from rocks. They plunge beneath the surface one hundred times a day, often collecting thirty pounds of shellfish. There is a shrine on this island that was built several centuries ago in honor of Ishigami, the goddess of the sea. She grants one wish in a lifetime to any female who comes to worship her. This tourist attraction is highlighted on the final page of the brochure, the gold lettering shimmering on the glossy paper. Edith is supposed to go there and make her one wish.

Edith slides the brochure beneath one of the pillows on the bed. She gets up and pours herself a cup of the steaming, woodsy tea. She decides that she prefers Jun's little notes to the brochure. She decides that she will go see them, the last ama divers on Kyushu. Who cares if they are a kitschy tourist attraction, not some secret she has to burrow into and peel back? The itching and burning on her skin has faded almost completely, but she can still feel something shifting and stretching within her. She misses her mother.

As she falls asleep, Edith tries to remember the taste of abalone, something she has eaten several times before. She tries to imagine Jun in bed with her, feeding her glistening chunks of abalone meat with his long fingers. But she can't place him in the bed. In her mind, she can't dress him in anything but the stiff, torturous polyester suit.

The next morning, he is at her door wearing a thin T-shirt and a tight, crisp pair of jeans. He looks younger and three-dimensional and full of too much that she could never tap into.

"My day off," he says, pushing a tray of tea at her. "We go today."

Edith holds the door open and clutches the robe to her chest as if he has never seen her in such attire.

"Of course," she says.

She doesn't know why she has said that. Of course. So formal. So stiff. Like the turning point in a melodramatic miniseries.

Edith stares at Jun's jawline and waits for a pulsing to start up somewhere in her body. She tries to imagine the outline and sinew of rounded muscle beneath his T-shirt and jeans. Jun waits in the hallway while she dresses. Are they pretending this is a dangerous expedition? Or merely a tourist's flimsy whim for some local color? Maybe Jun's personal tour is part of the resort package and Edith's little adventure will be charged to room 2446.

When Edith opens the door again, it is impossible to tell if Jun is being completely professional. If he's not interested in her at all or if he would make love to her if she simply took one or two steps back into the room and shifted her chin toward the unmade bed. Edith steps out into the hallway, wobbling between believing and not believing.

"Thank you," she says.

She has to look away then. He has to look away, too. Over and over, it is the same story for Edith. It is impossible to look in someone's eyes at the right moment. The exact moment.

EDITH's mother and all of Edith's aunts attended her fourth grade science fair. They stood together in a tight row, pushed up right next to Edith's display. During her demonstration, these women were not smiling and airy and cheesy, like usual. They were proud of Edith, and they were serious. Ferocious, even. Edith felt like the only kid in her entire family, as if there was no wild cohort of cousins banging around in her life. As if she were the only kid in the world. Edith was ashamed of her project, a simple baking soda and vinegar volcano. The brown playdough was dotted with her tiny fingerprints, an ugly blob instead of a mountain. Edith's mother and aunts watched intently as she poured in the vinegar. And as the foamy, cartoon-red lava fizzled, not even making it to the bottom of the pie pan, Edith had wanted to cry. She had wanted to apologize to these women standing before her and loving her so unabashedly and fiercely because she didn't like that feeling one bit. Edith likes to think that this is the moment when she realized her life's work. She feels most at home conducting her research alone on an atoll, spreading her small life out on those brittle coral islands that grew upward from the sea while at the same time a magnificent oceanic volcano sank down and down and out of this world.

THE women are not bare-chested and larger than life, like the ama on the cover of the tourist brochure. They are wearing wet suits, the top halves folded around their wastes like wilted, rubber flowers. White cotton tunics modestly hug their chests. There are four of them. They are huddled around a little fire in a ramshackle hut that's pushed into the jutting sea wall. The early-afternoon heat is suffocating, but Edith knows that these women have been diving in the cold water for hours already and are chilled to the bone.

Jun has led Edith into the little hut and perched her on an upside down bucket in a corner. He stands next to her without saying a word to either Edith or the group of women. Edith and Jun watch the women. He knows what they are saying. She does not. The women do not look at her. They chatter amongst themselves in low, quiet voices. They poke sticks into the fire and laugh often, easily. Edith feels like she should stand on her bucket and begin to perform something. Then they would shift and turn and watch her. That would be more comfortable than this—the staring. Finally Jun walks over to them and bows, smiling. They smile and nod back.

"Reiko is seventy-seven years old," Jun begins.

He walks down the line of them.

"Tazue is seventy-four. Mineyo is fifty-four. And Katsumi our baby. She is forty-three."

The women smile at Jun and laugh at this last bit, as if it is familiar and rehearsed.

The first woman points at her chest and says something in Japanese, smiling at Edith.

"Tazue say she wear only loin cloth when she was young," Jun says.

The women giggle.

"Now she wear wet suit and mask."

The next woman speaks, and Jun translates. They take turns giving out bits of information for the tourist.

We used to celebrate with red rice when a girl was born.

We begin when we are children. Gather kelp and seaweed on the beach.

We grow. We go further into the water.

We are told stories of the water.

Love, dragons, magic.

We cannot be greedy. When we are down there, if we want too much, we die.

Men do not dive because they need extra layer of fat, like us. They cannot do it.

(They all laugh at this, nudging at Jun playfully with their eyes.)

My daughter does not like the cold.

Our daughters and granddaughters do not want this work.
Diving ends soon.

The women watch Edith and smile at her when Jun is done translating. Perhaps they are waiting for her to ask questions. They do not seem uncomfortable in the silence. But to Edith, it is an open void. Now that she is out here on the island face to face with the missing puzzle piece in her family's lore, she can't think of a single thing to say. Her mother and her aunts would fill this hut with their silly awe and wonder and pride and joy, and Edith is silent. She has nothing. She should have called her mother before coming out here and pressed her for details. Was there a name attached to this ancestor? A story about a great grandfather meeting an island woman during the war? A love story? She has nothing, and she wonders if these women can see her deflating here in the tiny hut.

Edith tries to pull herself back into a specific memory of her mother or one of her aunts saying something about the ama story while the women in her family were in the kitchen chopping onion and garlic. Bucket-fulls, it seemed. Edith remembers that smell lingering on her mother's fingertips for days. She remembers staying up too late, reading something too serious in bed, and her mother quickly brushing at her bangs, that scent staying after she had left the room. In the kitchen, Edith's youngest aunt had once said something about the Japanese connection in passing, some random allusion to hard work and fortitude before moving on to gossip about the local swim club's female tennis league. And the statement had seemed quick and certain, as if this long-lost relative had just died in an upstairs bedroom, the idea of her still invoking hushed reverence and lazy awe as they chopped away. Each time one of the women in her family brought up the ama story, Edith's stomach would tighten. She couldn't pinpoint what, exactly, made her feel this way. But something felt forced. Something felt unfair. Yet here she is.

The women in the hut turn their attention back to the fire. Edith wants to ask them about her family's story, but there is no precise way to siphon it through the funnel of her memory and into Jun and finally to these women. No words or translation. Edith wishes she could simply make some solid gesture. She wishes she could shape the air with her hands in a way that would make all of that story suddenly appear. *Do you know her?* she could ask with her hands. *She is nameless. She is faceless. I don't think she ever existed. Could you push her forward, please?* As a child, Edith could have simply asked her mother for more information. Now she cannot.

The women push into the fire with their sticks and chat away in a language that sounds like solitude to Edith. She stands and nods toward Jun that she is ready to go. But then one of the women, the youngest, turns to Jun and asks him a question. He answers her.

"What was that?" Edith asks.

"She ask about my sister," Jun says. "In Tokyo now."

The youngest woman says something to Jun again, and he laughs.

"My sister try to dive," he tells Edith. "Katsumi say she too skinny."

"Your sister is an ama?"

"She try. She leave. She works in Tokyo. Can buy things she sees on television."

One of the women grabs Edith's hand and pulls her toward the fire. She crouches with them and the heat makes her feel itchy and out of control again.

"I sat in the boat," Jun says. "When my sister dives. I pull her up," he says. "Like a big fish."

Up close, Edith can see the damage from years of salt and sun on their faces, but also an odd kind of timelessness amid all that wear. The ama are roasting abalone in open shells over the fire. The juices spit and bubble around the white meat. The oldest woman offers a piece of meat that has cooled just enough. Edith takes it. She waits to recognize and remember the taste of the sea, but the meat is mild and tender, as empty as a clean white bowl.

Jun takes Edith to the shrine that is several yards from the ama hut. It is nothing more than a pile of rocks on an outcropping of the sea wall, pale, wind-worn flags flapping themselves at the Pacific.

"To look after dead ama-san," Jun says. "And killed whales."

If Edith squints just right, as she does at the fish in the aquarium at the bar, the pile of rocks and flags becomes something spectacular set against the open ocean. After being tucked within the artificial world of the Ocean Dome for so long, Edith can't help but be in awe now that she is finally standing at the precipice of the real thing. She is seeing and hearing and tasting the ocean for the first time. Her tourist self kicks into overdrive, and she can't help but think of the ama life as picturesque and quaint. Even danger and death are made melancholy and beautiful. She wants to tie a rough cord around her waist and hold her breath and dive down, Jun floating above her, singing in a boat. She wants to laugh about how men would be no good at this. She wants to join a secret matriarchy.

Jun points to the spot where Edith is supposed to kneel and make her silent wish to the goddess of the sea, her one wish in a lifetime. The pebbles press into her shins and knees and her excitement vanishes, sucked up by the roaring sea and the cutting wind. Although Edith knows that there is a wish inside of her—there are many—she feels only annoying emptiness. Nothing surfaces. She feels clean and white, like the taste of abalone. Scooped out. This moment, the entire trip, has already become a faded memory for Edith. Jun himself is soft around the edges and dissolving. Sex, Edith decides, would not change that. She will be back in Cleveland soon. The yellow stain around the bathtub drain. The crack in the kitchen windowpane. The small damp patch in the corner of her bedroom ceiling.

A woman wearing the same white cotton tunic as the ama divers approaches Edith and Jun as they leave. She holds out tiny bags that are emblazoned with stars and pentagrams.

"Ama lucky amulets," the woman says carefully. "Will keep you safe. I promise," she says. "I have been protected."

Edith buys three and then realizes that she did not get a chance to see the women dive. She is frustrated and angry with herself for not being able to ask those women a single thing, for not insisting that they take her out in the water with them. As they walk away from the shore, Edith stares at Jun's long arms and feels jilted, as if she has failed some secret test yet again. She came out here to the island of Kyushu to see the husbands and brothers sitting above the ama in little fishing boats. She came out here to see the weights strapped around the women's waists and the sharp little tools. But most of all, she came out here to hear the whistling sound that they make when they run through breathing exercises before a descent, the sound that has been described as hollow and haunting and sad. The first western sailors heard it hundreds of years ago and must have thought they had discovered the edge of the world, the very end. Edith thinks those women must be able to blow out sadness as if it isn't their own, as if it never could be. She had wanted to hear that.

EDITH wakes up in the middle of the night to knocking on her door.

"I show you something," Jun says, bowing.

He's in his bellhop uniform again. This signifies something, Edith decides in her tired state. This signifies that the two of them aren't going to make love or hold hands. That they won't even try.

But then Jun shrugs and smiles and purses his mouth with something like mischief.

"For you," Jun says, leading her to the elevator and then through the lobby and outside and finally he unlocks a little door at the back of the water park and ushers her in.

There is a feeling of familiarity, a warm thickness in the air between her body and Jun's. Edith feels like pushing her hand against her heart, holding herself steady.

"For you," Jun says again, flipping several switches on a wall panel in what looks like a sad break room.

He leads Edith through a few narrow, stuffy halls until suddenly they burst into the park where it is as bright as the middle of the day.

"You could get fired," Edith says, awake with her bare feet in the cool sand. "I could live here forever."

"Guinness Book of World Records. Three hundred meters long," Jun recites. "One hundred meters wide."

Edith wants to kiss him.

"The Ocean Dome closes soon. Not enough money."

The wave pool is still and smooth.

"It will be sad day," Jun says. "I will be sad."

In the harsh light, Edith sees Jun's eyes grow wet. It seems that the history of the water park, such an amazing feat, has overshadowed the story of the island itself. In her dreams, Edith would figure out a way to keep the park open, maybe only for herself. For centuries, scientists have been fascinated by how plants and animals have never truly learned how to leave the sea. We have all taken a bit of it with us. We've got that ancient water sloshing around inside of us, making so many living things anxious to return. Edith wants to learn the language. She wants to stay. She would shuffle the four women she met earlier that day away from the shore and seal them in here forever, a living museum. Jun, and even the women themselves, speak of the ama as if they are already gone. What if she could bring them here and they could become her life's work and they could live as if there is no other Japan or even world beyond the sliding dome sky? At night, parrot fish secrete beautiful envelopes of mucus in which they sleep, protected. Edith wants to wrap those women up in their own shimmery pockets and place them in the wave pool. Fringes of coral reef could rise up and form tiny islands that would protectively ring the sacred lagoon forever.

"Thank you," Edith says. "You could get fired."

"Please wait."

Jun disappears in the series of back hallways that led them here. There is a shifting clink above her. The lights dim into night. The base of the volcano rumbles. Fire spews, illuminating the plastic tube slides that snake through the foam rock. A circle of lime-green light flickers onto the hard wall of the horizon at the far end of the wave pool. The music pipes in, agitated techno.

"A show," Jun shouts as he walks back toward her. "For you."

One of the sunset laser light shows begins. Purples and pinks and yellows and blues skim the water and pierce the waves. There is a musty beach chair. Somehow, within the pulse of the music and the lights, Edith finds herself lying on that chair, Jun hovering above her once again. It is awkward when Jun shifts his weight next to her on the narrow chair. It is awkward when he reaches behind her shoulders to try to tilt the chair further back. Edith moves fast, pulling at Jun's pants and untucking his shirt. Jun touches her and makes her feel as if her skin has always been itchy and on fire and she has never been brave enough to admit it. But when the music shuts off, that lone circle of green light fixed on the far wall, they stop. They stand up and watch the waves die down and disappear. Edith turns to Jun and starts to tuck his shirt back in but then stops herself. She places her hands on his shoulders instead. She feels awkward once she has done this but she leaves her hands there anyway. Maybe Jun hadn't been expecting sex. Maybe there had just been that. She kisses him. He kisses her back, but the empty space between their two bodies pounds into her.

"Thank you," Edith says.

Jun nods toward the water.

"I haven't gotten in yet. Not once," Edith says.

Jun sits down, pressing his palms back behind him in the sand, his thick hair tousled. Edith walks to the edge of the shore and toes the warm water. Even as a kid, Edith has had this feeling when she touches any body of water: as if she will be sucked in to the center of the sea and down to the deepest buckles and folds of the ocean floor. Sitting on a dock and swinging her feet in the little river near her childhood home in Ohio, something waited beyond the sad, brown, polluted water. Edith has always felt something pulling her. She feels it in the Ocean Dome, a strange kind of sonar bouncing like mad off the walls of the water park. By the time she is waist deep, she wants the waves to start back up, intense, radioactive color shooting through them again. Edith wishes her cotton nightgown would bloom around her on the surface of the water, but it simply drags and clings, twisted up between her legs. She looks back at Jun, and he nods at the water again, as if it could have some ancient, mythical healing properties mixed in with the chlorine and everything else. As if he knows her. Without the distraction of the waves and the lights and the loud music and Jun pressed close, all Edith has is the lack of direction that is always with her. *I know nothing.* Edith wants to turn back to Jun and tell him this.

But Edith also feels good right now. She must admit this as she stands in that open pool. She has seen so much. She has seen a pipefish standing on its nose among blades of waving sea grass. She has been engulfed in clouds of metallic-blue wrasse and sweepers and silversides. Edith is certain that there have been moments in her life when she has been able to simply look at a thing without classifying it or pulling it apart. Right now as she stands here, dumb in the water, fingering the familiar, rounded edges of emptiness and longing in her mind, Edith finds comfort in what she knows she has seen. When she lived on that atoll in the middle of the Indian Ocean for five months, she pulled open a parrot fish that she had roasted over a fire and found jade green bones tucked into bright white flesh. Beauty without a purpose. Beauty just because.

Edith gropes for a vestige of the fever that is now completely gone. She longs to discover a random patch of hot, itchy skin. If only she could force a metamorphosis in the contained heat of the Ocean Dome. The light and the humidity and everything else could be calibrated just right, keeping this good feeling with her forever, waiting to usher her in.

Edith wants to believe something. She wants to start up the laser light show again and then believe that she could take Jun with her—or any man, really—beneath those sunset waves. That they could walk, holding hands, on the bottom of the fake ocean until they reached, somehow, the real thing. They could walk all the way into the deepest ocean trench where only magic exists.

It doesn't matter whether or not Jun joins Edith in the stagnant water of the pool. It doesn't matter whether or not anything more happens between them—if someone's mouth brushes up a bit awkwardly against an ear or the soft place just below a cheekbone, or if someone's hand blindly feels for something to hold onto. All Edith really wants is to imagine them exploring the fissures of the ocean floor. They could hold hands, beyond fear, imagining the first prehistoric fish before it stubbornly reappears right before their eyes.

the cellar

WE ARE OLD NOW.

Now, when we open the cellar door we know that there is more than just the fuse box and the wheezing dehumidifier and the dirt floor. Even before we flip the switch and stare down into the milky, weak light of the little bulb at the bottom of the stairs, we can tell. We spend time down there and ignore the mustiness and the draft. We wander the aisles and stop to touch the things on the shelves. We are always careful. Our favorites are the things in jars. There's the wedding ring that was lost in a Minnesota lake early in our marriage. We squint at the dull glint of it resting there at the bottom of the jar full of cloudy liquid. There is the first five dollar bill that we ever paid the babysitter. There is a recipe for the bread that we used to make every Sunday. The collar and tags of our second dog. A feather from a favorite down comforter floating weightless like a ghost.

We know that we are supposed to make something of these objects. We know that we are lucky to have them again, lined up in neat rows and labeled with little typewritten cards. They are here for us to gaze upon for hours if we wish, and we often do. There is no sense of urgency. Memory is a careful, rhythmic pulse at the base of our skulls when we spend time down here. There is no young or old. There is just this: the collection of our lives. Our once upon a time has become our relics. We stand in front of the series of jars that contain our children as infants. Maybe it seems grotesque. But it isn't. We stare at the folds of skin and fat that fall down their baby legs like the rings of a tree and re-member. Our children are grown and gone now. So it's nice to have this. It's nice to have the tiny toes and the pink lips again. The light in the cellar is dim and the fluid in the jars is milky. But still, we know that the pink is there all the same.

It's not just jars down here. There are a couple rows of glass display boxes, each one lit up softly from below. We found our first argument yesterday. We found the moment when we first met and stared at it for what felt like hours, watching it flicker and buzz. Seeing these things isn't anything at all like living them again. Early on, we talked about that for a while and made sure to make this clear to one another. It's a curiosity, that's all. There is a glass box at the end of one of the rows that contains a particu-larly passionate embrace. The edges are frayed with loose threads, but the color is still rich and vivid right at the center. There is a glass box full of lost keys.

We come down here. You'd be surprised by the pockets of warm air that can be found in an old cellar. How they can wash over two frail, close bodies like unexpected waves. How they can touch.

acknowledgements

The following stories, some of them in slightly different forms, first appeared in these journals:

"What You Are Now Enjoying," *Hayden's Ferry Review*
"Dear John," *Guernica*
"Careless Daughters," *Redivider*
"My Husband's House," *Copper Nickel*
"Vanishing Point," *The New Guard*
"Hank," *Orchid: A Literary Review*
"Wonder Woman Grew Up In Nebraska," *Small Spiral Notebook*
"The Cellar," *The Massachusetts Review*

Immense gratitude to the people who have helped shape the stories I tell. Thank you to my teachers, especially Barbara Bean, Stephanie Vaughn, Lamar Herrin, Maureen McCoy, Alison Lurie, and Dan McCall. Thank you to my story-telling friends who have shared couches and beers and laughter, laughter, laughter: Patrick Somerville, Siobhan Adcock, Jecca Hutcheson, Ann

Beauchner, and Theo Hummer. I am grateful for the support of the Bread Loaf Writers' Conference, the Ragdale Foundation, Pen Parentis, The Vermont Studio Center, and the Grub Street Launch Lab. Thank you to Janet Silver for agreeing that these stories needed to be told, and to all the folks at Autumn House who made that happen. Thank you to my students. Thank you to girlfriends who have held my world on their shoulders when necessary: Joy, Ali, and Shannon. My family, my heart: David, Janis, Amy, and Angie. Most of all, this book is for my husband and my two sons. Not only do you give me the time to tell my stories. You insist that they be told.

The Autumn House
Fiction Series

New World Order by Derek Green

Drift and Swerve by Samuel Ligon, 2008*

Monongahela Dusk by John Hoerr

Attention Please Now by Matthew Pitt, 2009*

Peter Never Came by Ashley Cowger, 2010*

Keeping the Wolves at Bay: Stories by Emerging American Writers, Sharon Dilworth, ed.

Party Girls by Diane Goodman

Favorite Monster by Sharma Shields, 2011*

Little Raw Souls by Steven Schwartz

What You Are Now Enjoying by Sarah Gerkensmeyer, 2012*

*Winners of the Autumn House Fiction Prize

design and production

Cover and text design: Chiquita Babb

Cover photo: iStockphoto

Author photo: Lori Deemer

Text set in Sabon, an oldstyle font designed by Jan Tschichold (1902–1974) between 1962 and 1967 and released in 1967. The roman face was based on types by Claude Garamond (c. 1480–1561); the italic face was based on types by a contemporary of Garamond, Robert Granjon.